pugs
in a
blanket

Also by J.J. Howard

Pugs and Kisses

Sit, Stay, Love

pugs
in a
blanket

j.j. howard

SCHOLASTIC INC.

Copyright © 2019 by Jennifer Howard

All rights reserved. Published by Scholastic Inc., *Publishers since 1920*. SCHOLASTIC and associated logos are trademarks and/or registered trademarks of Scholastic Inc.

The publisher does not have any control over and does not assume any responsibility for author or third-party websites or their content.

No part of this publication may be reproduced, stored in a retrieval system, or transmitted in any form or by any means, electronic, mechanical, photocopying, recording, or otherwise, without written permission of the publisher. For information regarding permission, write to Scholastic Inc., Attention: Permissions Department, 557 Broadway, New York, NY 10012.

This book is a work of fiction. Names, characters, places, and incidents are either the product of the author's imagination or are used fictitiously, and any resemblance to actual persons, living or dead, business establishments, events, or locales is entirely coincidental.

ISBN 978-1-338-33931-4

10 9 8 7 6 5 4 3 2 1   19 20 21 22 23

Printed in the U.S.A.   40
First printing 2019

Book design by Yaffa Jaskoll

For Nina

1

Don't Blame the Broccoli

"Only two more weeks of school—finally!" my best friend, Nina, announced as she stepped off the bus after me.

I looked over at her, surprised. "*I'm* usually the one counting down to summer vacation," I said. "You love school."

She sighed. "Yeah. I'm just really excited to go to California!"

Now it was my turn to sigh. Thanks to my parents' catering business, my family almost never went on trips. Since cooking was my favorite thing in the world, I didn't mind helping out at our events. But sometimes I did feel jealous of all the traveling Nina's family did.

"I *will* miss Monster and Molly when we go," Nina said as we walked down the street together.

I felt another sigh escape—I was *also* jealous of the fact that Nina had not just one but two adorable dogs. I'd been asking for a puppy for Christmas or my birthday or Arbor Day—I wasn't picky—since I was six. But my mother was firmly anti-dog. Well, she was anti-anything that got in the way of working on events for Calloway's Creations.

"Too bad I can't dog-sit for you," I said, adjusting my backpack on my shoulder. It was a typically hot May afternoon in West Palm Beach, Florida.

"I know," Nina agreed. "I hate that M and M have to stay at the vet's. I even asked my parents if I could bring them with us."

I laughed out loud as I pictured Monster—a Great Dane—and Molly—a Siberian husky—trying to fit under an airplane seat.

"Sam, I wish *you* could have a dog," Nina told me, lifting her long brown hair off the back of her neck.

I nodded sadly, looking down at my green sandals. "I just

have to keep asking. Summer would be a great time to get a puppy—I'd be home from school so I could train him or her."

"Good point. You can put that on your list."

I glanced up. "My list?"

Nina raised one eyebrow. "You've never compiled a comprehensive list to present to your parents of reasons you should have a pet? Have I taught you nothing?"

I laughed. "Can you picture getting my mom to stand still long enough to read a list like that?" I shook my head. "Not unless it was a grocery list for an event."

Nina put her arm around me sympathetically. "You're right," she said. "It's pretty much food twenty-four seven at your house, I know." She paused. "Hey, do you have a new recipe in the works?" Nina loved being a taste tester for my cooking creations.

I smiled with anticipation as we rounded the corner. "I've been thinking of two new dishes. One's a spicy chicken meatball and the other is a roasted broccoli side."

"Yum on the meatballs, but you can keep the broccoli." Nina crinkled her nose. "My dad makes it all the time, and . . . yuck."

I chuckled, remembering the last time I'd been at the Katzif house for dinner. "You can't blame the broccoli," I said. "Your dad just boils all the flavor out and then puts cheese on top. If you treat it right, broccoli is super delicious. It's my second-favorite cruciferous vegetable!"

Nina rolled her eyes and laughed. "Only you, Sam Calloway, could get so excited defending the honor of a vegetable." We reached the corner of Nina's street and she turned and waved. "Text me later!"

"Okay. Later, friieeeennnndd!" Nina and I had a tradition of calling each other *friend* but drawing out the word so that it lasted as long as possible.

"Bye, friieeeen . . ." Nina's voice trailed off as she headed down her street.

I hitched my backpack higher on my shoulder and walked over to my town house on the next block. I reached into the front pocket of my backpack for my key, but then I realized that our porch gate was unlocked. I knew right away that it was my little brother, Oliver's, fault. His elementary school gets out before my middle school, and our parents' van and car were both missing, so they weren't home yet. Ollie knows he's supposed to lock the gate; Mom, Dad, and I have all reminded him one million times. But still, he always forgets.

I was halfway across the porch when I heard it: a whimpering sound.

I froze.

After a quick look around, I didn't see anything out of place. Maybe I'd just heard a squirrel in a nearby tree. But then the sound came again. It was definitely a whimper, and this time I could tell that it was coming from a big cardboard box that was sitting on one of the lounge chairs. At first I hadn't even noticed the box. Now I wondered if it was some sort of delivery of catering supplies for my parents.

I walked over to the box and peered inside. And I couldn't believe what I saw.

2

Three Wishes?

Inside the box were two little dogs, wrapped up in a pink-and-white-striped blanket. When they saw me, they both started whimpering and trying to wriggle out of the blanket.

The dogs were pugs. I was sure of that. A girl in my school has a pug that comes with her dad in the car when she gets picked up. Pugs have wrinkly little old-man faces and huge black eyes, and they're absolutely adorable.

Exactly like these two dogs.

I unwound the blanket and stroked each dog on the head. Their ears were velvety soft.

"Where did you two come from?" I asked.

Two sets of big black eyes blinked up at me. One of the pugs gave a short bark, as though trying to answer my question.

I was still in shock. Why were there two dogs on my porch? It seemed like Nina's wish for me had just magically come true— times two. Was my best friend secretly a magical genie or something? Did I still have two wishes left? If so, I decided on the spot that I'd wish to keep the dogs—and also to be tall.

I patted the talkative one on the head once more. "Stay right here," I told the pugs.

I walked back out of the porch gate and checked the parking area. But no one was around. Not knowing what else to do, I returned to the box of pugs, picked it up, and carried it inside the house with me. It was too hot for these little guys to be outside—with a blanket, no less! They were both panting, their pink tongues hanging out of their mouths.

"Ollie!" I yelled as I stepped into the foyer, but got no answer. I shut the door behind me and glanced at the dry-erase board on the fridge. My little brother had scrawled one word: *Colin*, which meant he'd walked over to his best friend's house. Someone must have left these little guys on the porch after Ollie had left for Colin's.

I looked back down at the dogs and examined them more closely. Neither wore a collar, and there was nothing in the box with them except the blanket. No note or anything. So strange.

Immediately, one of the dogs began to bark frantically and hop around inside the box. Oh no. What if he or she had to go to the bathroom? Or rather, go *outside*, I corrected myself. Dogs didn't use bathrooms.

Keeping the blanket tucked under the pug—just in case—I carried the dog back outside and set him down at the curb. He lifted his leg to go, so then I knew he was a boy dog.

I decided it was a good idea to take the other dog out, too. She turned out to be a girl dog. I wondered if they were brother and sister. They did look a lot alike, but the boy was definitely a bit rounder in the middle.

Back in the house, I set the two pugs down in the living room and got them a little dish of water, which they lapped right up. I watched as they ran around, sniffing the rug and barking happily. It was so surreal. Why had the dogs been left on our porch? Had someone meant to leave them on a different porch, but got confused? That seemed possible; all the town houses in our neighborhood looked pretty much exactly alike.

When in doubt, text your BFF. But first, take a picture.

I pulled out my phone and tried twice to get both pugs in the same frame, but they were too wriggly. I finally gave up and texted Nina a picture of the girl pug and part of the boy's head. Since Nina was the smartest person I knew, maybe she'd know what to do.

She texted back right away:

OMG HOW CUTE! WHOSE R THEY???

No clue. Found on our porch. Just me at home—HELP!?!

Wait wait—what??? I JUST wished for a dog for you. Maybe I am magic? Am checking mailbox now 4 my Hogwarts letter!!!!

Haha save room for me in Hufflepuff. But seriously what should I do?

Sorry I'm going Slytherin all the way. But if they're lost—post a sign maybe? On that bulletin board by yr mailboxes?

Good idea. Can u come over to help me?

☹ nope. Lax game in 15. Text me later w/an update??

Just then, I heard the porch gate swing open. Mom! Without even thinking I picked up first one dog and then the other. I placed them gently back in the box and ran upstairs to my room with the box in my arms.

I'd made a little reading nook on one side of my closet—our town house is pretty small so privacy is hard to come by. So I set down the box in the empty space in the closet and then stood back. I wondered if the pugs could climb out of the box. It was pretty tall, and their legs were pretty short. But I still had no idea.

"Can you guys just be chill for a few until I figure out what to do?" I asked them. My heart was racing. I needed more time to figure out a plan!

I swear both dogs looked me straight in the eyes, their expressions serious. It even seemed as if the boy dog bobbed his head once up and down, as though he were nodding.

"Sam!"

I heard Mom calling my name, so I pulled the door to my room shut and took off running back down the stairs.

I came to a rapid stop at the foot of the stairs and reminded myself to act casual. "Oh, hello there, Mother. I see that you're home now. Glad to see . . . I mean, welcome home!"

I have this thing where I can't stop talking when I'm nervous.

Mom was unpacking a canvas bag of groceries. She paused with a bag of pasta in midair and raised her eyebrows. "Okay, weird, but thanks. Why are you panting?"

"I'm not *panting*!" I argued. Had Mom somehow peeked inside my mind and seen the image of the panting pugs in there?

Mom narrowed her eyes at me. "Sam? What's going on?"

I frowned. This acting casual thing was off to a very bad start.

I decided to try a different tactic. "So anyhow, I'm ready to get cooking!" I said brightly. "What are we prepping for the event tomorrow?"

Menu planning was always a sure bet for distracting my mother.

"Pretty standard apps, and then a choice of trout amandine or beef Wellington for the main."

I made an exaggerated snoring sound. "Ugh, so boring. That's like a nineteen eighties menu."

"Try nineteen fifties. But it's what they wanted. It's the Wilkersons' anniversary party. They call the shots."

"I hope you at least tried to sell them on something a little snazzier. Maybe some spicy chicken meatballs?" I suggested hopefully.

"Sam, you know it's about what the client wants."

"That's why I'm going to have my own restaurant when I get older."

"I'm sure you will," Mom said as she pulled out the big cutting board and laid a huge bag of celery on top of it. "Just remember, that's not an easy side of the business, either. I can tell you that from experience. For now, how about you jump in and start chopping up this celery?"

"We're not seriously making cream-cheese-stuffed celery?" I cocked my head to the side and gave her a look.

"Sam, I told you, it's what the customer wants."

I picked up a bunch of celery and began to pull apart the stalks. "But it's so ordinar—" Just then, one of the dogs upstairs gave a short bark. The sound was muffled, but Mom definitely heard it.

"What was that?" she asked with a frown.

I held up the celery, which was a conveniently loud food when snapped. "Celery."

Mom narrowed her eyes. "Okay . . . but why did you just stop in the middle of *complaining* about the celery?"

I shrugged. "I guess it's not so bad." I set down the celery stalk. "Um. I'll be right back. I have to . . . go to the bathroom."

When Mom wasn't looking, I swiped a foil-wrapped square of cream cheese from the counter, shoved it under my T-shirt, and ran upstairs toward my room.

"Why are you going upstairs?" The sound of Mom's voice followed me. It was a valid question since we had a downstairs bathroom right near the kitchen.

Halfway up, I turned, still balancing the cream cheese under my top. "Um, I need to get some lip balm, too, and it's in my room. Be back soon!" I ran the rest of the way upstairs before she could say any more or I had to tell any more lies about celery or lip balm.

Once in my room, I opened the door quietly, hoping not to spook the dogs.

"I'll be right there, guys," I whispered into the closet. Then I went to my bathroom sink and carefully unwrapped the small block of cream cheese. I broke off two chunks and headed back to the pugs. The boy was standing up on his hind legs with his front paws on the side of the box. The girl was curled up in a ball, but glanced up at me expectantly. The box was already looking pretty rough.

I held out a hand with a ball of cream cheese for each pug, giggling (quietly!) at the sensation of the dogs' wet tongues tickling my fingers.

"What am I doing?" I asked the dogs as they ate eagerly. I felt the urge to text Nina again, but she was at lacrosse, and my texting hand was currently covered in cream cheese and dog saliva.

Mom was always on edge the day before an event. Maybe if I just stalled until tomorrow's event was over, I could tell her about the dogs *then* without her freaking out. I was afraid that she'd say no right away to us keeping the dogs, even if it was just until we figured out who they belonged to. As I studied their cute faces, I knew I couldn't stand the thought of these pups going to a dog shelter. I kept thinking of those commercials with the sad music and the even sadder dogs' faces as they stared at the camera from behind the bars of what looked like doggy jail.

In the meantime, I decided as the dogs finished their very thorough licking, I would follow Nina's advice and make signs to put up on the community bulletin board.

Each pug had eaten their blob of cream cheese, so I whispered to the dogs, "I'll be back in a few minutes. You guys have a nap, okay?" I blew them each a kiss (sticky hands meant no head pat) and hurried into the bathroom to wash my hands.

I peered into my mirror and groaned when I saw my messy ponytail had come undone again. Mom says my hair is strawberry blonde, which I like because strawberries are my third favorite fruit. But my hair is straight and really fine, so it's always sliding out of ponytail holders and barrettes. I sighed, fixed my hair, and splashed some water on my pale skin, which absolutely resists getting tan. At least I like my green eyes, though, since they aren't a typical eye color.

I wrapped up what remained of the cream cheese, hid it in my shirt again, and ran back downstairs. I'd already been gone pretty long and Mom would be suspicious.

Luckily, though, when I got back to the kitchen, Mom seemed to be pretty intent on sautéing some onions, so I jumped back into my celery chopping.

When the onions had caramelized, Mom took the pan off the heat, and in the sudden quiet, one of the dogs made a kind of squeaking sound. Mom's head shot up and swiveled toward me.

"Excuse me!" I said quickly, and much too loudly, patting the top of my chest. "Hiccups," I added, then made a noise—my best impression of a combination of the pug's squeak and an actual hiccup.

This earned me an even more confused look from my mother. "Sam. Was that a hiccup or have you been possessed? Seriously, what is *with* you today?"

"Nothing!" I said, too quickly. "What's with you?"

"Nice try. Are you done with the celery?"

"Almost," I said, breaking apart the last stalk and starting to chop.

"Hey, what happened to the rest of this cream cheese?" Mom picked up the opened block I'd taken upstairs.

It wasn't hard to pretend to look guilty. "Sorry. I guess I got hungry."

Mom cocked her head to the side as she stared at me. I waited, tense, for her to say *I know you're hiding dogs upstairs!* But Mom surprised me.

"I'm sorry, Sam," she said, her voice soft. "You've been at school all day and I'm sure you're tired. Nothing I need to prep ahead is very interesting—but it's also pretty easy stuff. You go upstairs and take a break like a regular kid. Give Nina a call or something."

Well, at least my weird behavior had given me an out to go pug-sit upstairs. "Mom, that's silly," I told her. "We don't use our phones to *call* each other."

Mom rolled her eyes. "Smarty-pants." She handed me two stalks of celery. "Balance out all that cheese you ate," she ordered.

"Thanks, Mom."

Now I had to figure out what to do with these two gross, plain stalks of celery.

Oh, and also with the two pugs hidden in my room.

3

Triple Threat

I stayed in my room with the dogs all evening, trying to keep them quiet by distracting them with a balled-up pair of socks (which they promptly began chewing on). I wished I had some *real* dog toys. Thankfully, the girl dog eventually curled up and took a nap, snoring away cutely. After a little while, her brother joined her and they slept peacefully in their box.

That gave me time to escape downstairs for dinner (and to sneak the celery into the trash). Ollie, it turned out, was sleeping over at Colin's for the weekend, and wouldn't be coming to the event tomorrow. This was lucky for me—one less person to evade. And Mom, exhausted from all the food prep, announced she was going to bed early. Dad said he was tired, too. Whew.

My parents went upstairs to their bedroom. I waited until their door was closed, and then I raced up to my room. The pugs were wide awake and standing up in the box; their little tails began wagging the minute I appeared.

"Keep quiet," I whispered to them. I picked them up, holding each one under my arm, and snuck them downstairs. As silently as possible, I opened the front door and took the pugs outside so they could do their business again.

Back in my room, with the pugs stashed once more in their box with a bowl of water, I started making a flyer. The small photo printer my mom had gotten me for Christmas finally came in handy. I snapped a pic of the two dogs (they managed to be in the same frame this time). Then I typed: FOUND: TWO PUGS! WHO DO THEY BELONG TO? PLEASE CONTACT SAM C. I included my phone number and printed out the sheet.

I tiptoed outside to hang up the flyer on the bulletin board by the community mailboxes; everyone who lived in the town houses on our block would see the flyer when they went to check their mail. I'd just have to be sure to beat my parents to the mailbox when we got home from the event tomorrow—unless someone called to claim the dogs before then.

As I returned to my house, I frowned at the thought of having to give up my little wish dogs so soon. But if their true owner called, at least they wouldn't go to a shelter—and be separated . . . or worse.

Back in my room, I set my alarm to get up super early—even before my mom on an event day, which meant four forty-five a.m. Then I crawled into bed and whispered "Good night" to the pugs, who were both sound asleep in their box again. I only hoped they wouldn't bark in the middle of the night and wake my parents; I probably wouldn't be able to come up with an excuse for *that*.

"Hey, pups," I whispered when my alarm went off the next morning. Thankfully, they hadn't barked at all in the night, but they were up now, wriggling around in their box. "Time to go do your business," I said, getting out of bed.

I wiped my sleepy eyes before taking first the more vocal boy dog, and then the girl dog, downstairs to go outside. I didn't trust my tired feet to carry them both down at one time. On our way back inside, I snagged some peanut butter from the kitchen to feed them.

With the pugs stashed back in my room eating, I showered and changed. Then I joined my parents for breakfast, trying to act normal. Luckily, my parents were so frantic prepping for the upcoming event they didn't pay close attention to me.

My parents' distraction *also* allowed me to sneak the dogs' box into the back of the catering van at the last minute, with Dad already at the wheel and Mom in the passenger seat. I knew that once we got to the event, everything would be even more chaotic, and my parents would be too busy to notice much of anything. Hopefully.

As we drove to the event, I realized I couldn't keep up this dog-hiding scam much longer. If I didn't get a text or a call about the pugs today, I'd pretty much have to fess up to my parents.

The Wilkerson party was being held at an event center we'd been to at least a hundred times before—definitely not the most exciting place in West Palm Beach. But at least it was familiar. I knew of a shady spot near the building where I could hide the pugs but still check on them regularly.

While my parents were busy carrying trays of food into the building, I grabbed the doggy box from the van and hurried it over to the shady nook. I felt bad leaving the pugs in the box all day, but I had no other way of making sure they stayed put. I just hoped that neither of them could or would crawl out of it. They hadn't done so yet, so that gave me hope, at least. Before I left them, I filled up a little sauce container with water in case they got thirsty. Then I patted their heads, whispered "I'll be back soon," and headed off.

I hurried into the event space. I could hear my parents setting up in the kitchen that was behind a pair of swinging doors. A few workers were putting down a small dance floor and others were hanging up streamers. The stage was already set up and I recognized the event singer, who goes by the name Dr. Jams (which is short for his real last name, Jambagi—although I'm pretty sure the *doctor* part is made up). Dr. Jams performs at a lot of the same events that Calloway's Creations caters. I know all the words to most of the song covers he usually sings. The other day in the car Ollie and I spontaneously started singing a Billy Idol song that came out way before we were born, and we only knew it because of Dr. Jams.

From across the room, I thought I saw Dr. Jams standing at the microphone, singing a few bars. But when I got closer I did a double take. It wasn't Dr. Jams. Even though the guy standing there sounded like him and looked like him, he was actually a boy maybe my age or a little older. He was just really tall.

I jumped in surprise as I heard the real Dr. Jams's voice behind me.

"Hi, Sam, how've you been?" he asked.

"Pretty good, Dr. Jams. I haven't seen you for a couple weeks."

"Took some time off. Say, have you met my son, Jai?" He gestured to the boy onstage, who was already jumping off the platform and holding out his hand for me to shake. "This is Sam Calloway. Sam, my son, Jai."

"Hi," I said, shaking his hand back.

"Ah, Calloway's Creations." Jai grinned. "I've definitely eaten some of their delicious leftovers," he added, patting his stomach.

"Me too," I told him. "I mean, I think I'm mostly made of leftovers." Some weeks it seemed that was all we ever ate—extra food from some event or other. You might think that having a chef for a mom would mean eating really well all the time. But by the time Mom gets done with cooking for work, she never wants to do *more* cooking at home. That was actually how I'd started cooking: by making new dinners for our family.

Jai (his name rhymed with *hi*) laughed at my leftover joke, which made me like him right away. He had brown skin just a bit lighter in tone than his father's and his eyes were an unusual color: a brown so light they almost looked gold.

I realized Dr. Jams was talking to me and I snapped to attention. ". . . so Jai is going to be living with me for the summer, and he's quite the performer, so you'll probably be seeing him around. Isn't that right, son?"

Jai nodded. "I go to a school for performing arts at home. I mean, in Maryland."

"Jai is an amazing singer and dancer. And actor. He is—what do you call that again?"

"A triple threat," Jai and I answered in unison. Dr. Jams laughed.

"That's cool," I said. "My school has a big performing arts program, so some of my friends are into music and acting and stuff." I paused, then added, "Not me, though. I'm all about the culinary arts."

"Oh," Dr. Jams said. "Maybe Jai should come check out your school, Sam."

"I'm just visiting," Jai said.

I thought I caught a hint of some tension coming off of Jai at his dad's excitement over my school. But then Jai asked me, "So you want to be a chef?"

"I do," I said. "I love cooking."

"Sam is already a chef," Dr. Jams put in. "Some of those leftovers you liked so much were made by her, I guarantee."

"Thanks, Dr. Jams," I said, my cheeks warming up.

"Sam, please, call me Devesh. Dr. Jams is just my stage name, you know."

I nodded, but then I froze when I thought I heard the sound of barking coming from outside.

Oh no.

"Uh-oh," I said. "I have to go check on . . . something."

Before Dr. Jams or Jai could ask me what was wrong, I'd turned on my heel and dashed away. I sprinted past my parents, who were setting up the buffet, and straight toward the shady spot where I'd hidden the dogs.

Both pugs were barking, standing on their hind legs and trying to scramble out of the tall box. I picked up the girl first and made a move to pick up the boy, but the girl dog was wriggling around too much.

I didn't realize Jai had followed me until I heard him make an "aww" sound.

I turned around, my heart jumping, one pug trying to scramble out of my arms. I guess I was caught. But at least there were no parents around.

"Do you want some help?" Jai offered.

I nodded enthusiastically and handed him the dog I'd picked up, who had quieted down. I reached into the box to scoop up the other—the boy dog. I really needed to give them names. But if I gave them names, I knew it would be even harder to give them back when we found the rightful owner.

"How old are they?" The pug in his arms licked his face and Jai laughed.

"No idea. I just found them yesterday on our porch." The pug I held let out a *yip* sound, as if in agreement.

"Oh wow," Jai said. "Are you going to keep them?"

"I don't think so," I said. "I mean, I'm trying to find the owner. Maybe someone left them there by mistake." I sighed, then glanced toward the tent. "Besides, I'm not allowed to have a dog. Or dog*s*."

"That's too bad," Jai said with a frown. "Dogs are awesome."

The pug in my arms dug his paws into my shoulder, and it tickled. "Do you have a dog?" I asked Jai.

He nodded. "Back home . . . he's with my mom right now. His name is Dipper."

"Oh my gosh—from *Gravity Falls*?" I asked.

Jai's face lit up. "Yeah! Not everyone gets that reference. I really loved that show."

"Me too." I felt myself grinning back. "What kind of dog is he?"

"A whole bunch of kinds—he's a mutt. He's kind of medium-sized. I don't think Dipper was *ever* this little." Jai scratched the pug's belly and she gave a contented sigh.

"Sam!" The sound of my mom's bellow gave me a start, and I reluctantly tucked the boy pug back into the box.

"I have to go," I told Jai.

"Same. My dad will be looking for me." Jai handed me back the other dog and I set her down beside her brother.

Jai and I walked back to the tent together. "Do you come to a lot of these party things?" Jai asked me. "I'm going to be helping my dad this summer."

I nodded. "Yeah, I almost always help my parents." The idea of having Jai around at future events made me smile.

When we entered the tent, Jai headed back toward the stage, and I headed toward the food prep area.

"Okay, well, bye for now, Sam," Jai said, waving.

"Bye, Jai," I said, then added, "Oh, can I ask you a favor?"

Jai turned, raising his eyebrows. "Sure. What's up?"

"Don't say anything about the pugs outside," I whispered. "They're . . . a secret. For now."

Jai nodded. "Your secret is safe with me."

The whole party was going smoothly. I hadn't heard the pugs bark. Dr. Jams and Jai were performing to much applause. And the Wilkersons and their guests seemed to be having a great time.

But then came time to serve the main course.

"Sam, we're shorthanded tonight," Mom told me in the hot kitchen. "I need your help to serve the mains." Her voice had the frantic tone I knew so well.

"Sure," I said.

Mom handed me two plates of beef Wellington. I followed the other servers—Kate and another woman I didn't know; she must have been new. My parents usually hired the same folks to help out with their events.

The three of us reached a round table of six and I waited for Kate's small nod before lowering my plates to the diners in front of me. You're supposed to serve everyone at the table at the same time if possible.

I went back to the kitchen and got two more plates, then two more, but one of the plates from the final pair turned out to be an extra.

And that's when I made a bad decision. I thought the pugs would probably enjoy a few bites of beef Wellington. And it was time for them to have lunch, anyway. So I snuck outside with the extra plate and deposited it in the box between the two wriggly pugs.

The dogs were thrilled. They immediately started chowing down, and I smiled at their wagging tails as they ate. Between them, the two dogs ate every scrap of the meaty treat. When they were finished, I patted their heads and went back into the building with the licked-clean plate. I had just another hour to go, and then I could bring the pugs back home. I felt really bad keeping them in the box; it was time to let them be free.

The pugs must have had the same idea. And they must have smelled that there was more beef Wellington out there in the party.

Because a few minutes later, after I'd returned to the kitchen, I heard a crash and a scream from out in the main room.

Mom, Dad, the servers, and I all rushed out to see what the commotion was. I already had a bad feeling in the pit of my stomach, though.

And there, in the middle of the Wilkersons' anniversary party, were the pugs. Somehow, finally, they had managed to escape their box. Now they stood on their hind legs at the table closest to the door, inching their noses toward the plates of beef Wellington. One shocked diner had dropped her water glass, and there were murmurs of surprise all around.

Everyone could see that the beef Wellington crumbs all over the dogs' faces explained their fervor to run into the party to try to find more tasty food.

My mother was the one who could spot the guilty look on *my* face, though.

The music stopped and I glanced toward the stage. Jai looked at me with wide eyes.

The real triple threat of the evening turned out to be: hungry pugs, beef Wellington, and me.

* * *

The ride home from the Wilkerson party seemed to take forever. Mostly because no one dared say anything after Mom snapped, "We'll talk about this when we get home." Neither Dad nor I were inclined to test her out, but I did appreciate the sympathetic look Dad gave me before he got behind the wheel of the van.

Since the dogs had pretty much destroyed their box while escaping it, I'd recycled it at the event space. Now I tried to balance both pugs on my lap as we rode. They just barely fit. Luckily, their bellies were full of tasty beef and pastry, so they both fell asleep. Their quiet snores were the only sounds in the van.

I guess Mom was waiting to interrogate me under bright lights. As soon as we got home, she flipped on the overhead fluorescent kitchen light, then gestured for me to take a seat at our small table.

"I have to take them out first," I told her, nodding down to the pugs I held in my arms. They'd woken up when I'd taken them out of the car, and were squirming around. Things would be so much worse if one or both of them made a mess in the house.

"Go ahead," Dad said, holding the door open for me.

The pugs did their business, and I brought them back inside. Dad had retrieved an old blanket—one we used to take to the beach—and spread it out on the kitchen floor. I put first one and then the other pug down on the blanket, and luckily they seemed content to stay there—and go back to snoring.

Mom pointed at them. "Explain."

I sat down at the table across from her and took a deep breath. "I found them."

"Where?" Mom demanded. "And since when do we bring animals that we just . . . find to an *event*?"

"Your mom is right, Sam," Dad said gently, taking a seat at the table with us. "Luckily, the Wilkersons had a good sense of humor about the whole thing. But a mishap like that could cost us business in the future."

"I'm sorry," I said, twisting my hands in my lap. "Really." I swallowed. "It's just . . . I found the dogs on our porch. Yesterday. After school."

"*Yesterday?*" Mom cried, and I flinched. I knew she wouldn't take that well.

"You've been keeping them a secret for almost twenty-four hours?" Dad asked, sounding stunned.

"I know, I know." I held up my hands in defeat. "It was wrong. I didn't tell you, I mean . . . *yet*, because, well, I thought . . . I just wanted to see if I could find out who they really belonged to before you . . ." I glanced up at Mom. "Before they had to go to a shelter. I was afraid they would be separated. Or, you know . . . something worse."

Mom didn't say anything right away, but I saw her realize what I really meant. She still looked angry, but her expression had changed somehow. Like maybe she was feeling a little bit sad, too. But she still sounded mad when she finally said, "I see. You assumed that your heartless mother would cart them off to an animal shelter right away, no questions asked."

"No—I didn't assume. I was just afraid . . ."

Mom frowned. "How did I become Cruella de Vil in this scenario?"

"You're not! But I . . ."

"Hold on a moment—both of you," Dad jumped in. Probably

he was afraid we were both about to say stuff we'd regret later. It wouldn't be the first time he'd played peacemaker between the two of us. "Sam, you shouldn't have hidden the dogs. Not telling us is essentially lying, and whatever your motives, we don't lie to each other in this house. But it's late and we're all tired from the event." He turned to Mom. "Let's figure out consequences tomorrow. And we'll decide then what to do about those two." He glanced at the pugs and I thought I saw a small smile cross his face—it *was* hard to deny their cuteness. Couldn't Mom see that, too? "Either way, they're stuck with us for the night," Dad finished, turning back to us.

"Fine," Mom said, her voice flat. She was definitely really mad at me. "Sam, take the dogs to sleep in your room for the night. And get them some water. But be sure to take them out first thing in the morning. I don't want any messes."

I wanted to tell her that I'd already successfully cared for the dogs for one night, but I thought it best not to remind her of that.

She walked past me and up the stairs. I gave Dad a grateful look, but he wouldn't meet my eyes.

I decided to focus on the dogs.

I brought them and the blanket upstairs, and settled them on the floor of my room. I was glad that at least they no longer had to stay inside that old box, or in my closet. They were awake now, but seemed relaxed.

I sat down on the floor to say good night to them. The boy dog kept staring at me with his round black eyes, which seemed so wise somehow.

"Where did you come from, little boy?" I asked him. He stared back intently, as though he wanted to answer me. If only he could speak, and tell me why the two of them had been left on our porch . . . and whether or not anybody might come back for them.

"How about you?" I asked his sister. She only stared back, too, her little tail wagging.

I sighed, kissed each of them on their soft furry heads, and stood up. I crawled into my bed, but within a few minutes the girl dog started making soft crying sounds. I gave up and brought first her and then the boy up on my bed with me.

Mom would freak. But, I figured, I was already in trouble. What could one more mistake matter?

The girl dog quieted and soon they both curled up next to me. I lay awake for a while, listening to their little hearts beating, and replaying the disastrous scene at the event over and over in my mind. But, snuggled in beside the two warm dogs, eventually I fell asleep.

4

Team Dog

The boy dog was snuggled close to my head, right beside my pillow, when I woke up the next morning. His big, round black eyes stared into mine and then he gave me a sloppy, wet kiss right on the side of my face. My heart melted and I hugged him.

But then everything that had happened the night before came rushing back to me and I felt almost sick. I wasn't used to getting in trouble. And then another, even more terrible thought occurred to me: Today might be the last day I'd get to spend with this little guy and his sister.

I felt a bit like crying, but I tried to push past it. I sat up and swung my legs over the side of the bed. As soon as I did, both pups were in motion, and I barely got the chance to lift them back down onto the floor. I didn't want them to jump and hurt themselves. After all, they weren't cats that would always land on their feet, and their legs were very short.

I wished I could stay in my room and avoid facing my mom for as long as possible, but one thing I'd already learned was that when you have dogs in your room, you're not sleeping in late or hanging out. First the boy and then the girl started pawing my legs. They looked up at me with their tongues hanging out the sides of their mouths, panting. The boy gave a short bark. It was time to go out.

I carried them downstairs, one tucked under each arm, going carefully down the stairs in my bare feet.

Mom was making coffee in the kitchen as I walked past. I didn't know what to say or do. It seemed too early to jump into "I'm sorry," especially with two armfuls of wriggly, needing-to-go-outside pug. So, I settled for "Good morning."

I got a nod back, which did not seem like a good sign, but I had a job to focus on, so I took the dogs out. The whole process would be so much easier if I had leashes for them. But then, we wouldn't need leashes if we ended up taking them to a shelter. We could use another box for that. I swallowed past the new lump in my throat and took the pugs back inside. At least it was Sunday, and I'd learned from Googling around that most nearby shelters were closed today.

Mom was sitting at one of the stools at the kitchen island, sipping her coffee.

"Have a seat." She gestured to my usual chair at the kitchen table. The pugs were clamoring around me—probably hungry— but since the low point of this dog adventure so far had come from my feeding them the beef Wellington, I tried to ignore them.

"I'm really sorry. About hiding the dogs," I began.

Mom frowned. "I know you are. Honestly, Sam, I'm more surprised than anything. You've always been so reliable."

"I try to be! But I found these two and I guess I just went a little . . . dog crazy. You know how much I've always wanted a dog," I added.

Mom nodded. "I know you have. And you know the reasons why it's not a great idea for us as a family."

"I would take care of them."

"Sam—you're really getting ahead of yourself. First of all, these dogs were obviously left here by mistake. We have to try to find their rightful owner. Second, hiding the dogs from me and your father—which caused a huge ruckus at our event—isn't exactly the best way to start convincing us that you're responsible enough to have a pet."

"I put up a flyer on the bulletin board," I told her. "I mean, for the first part you said—I do know that we need to look for the owners."

Mom blinked in surprise. "Oh. I didn't know you did that. Although that's more sneaking around that you did, so I'm not praising it," she added. "But it is a good start as far as finding the owners."

She got up and poured herself more coffee. "I've been thinking about this all night," she went on. Mom hadn't slept? Now I felt even worse. "Sam, you've always been so helpful with Calloway's Creations. You do so much, especially for someone your age—and you almost never complain. So the fact that you did this drastic thing—hiding the dogs—says to me that you must have felt that you had a good reason. I guess you really *were* worried I'd just dump the dogs at a shelter so we could get back to work."

I opened my mouth—maybe to argue with her—but then I shut it again. That was pretty much exactly what I'd been afraid would happen.

Mom smiled sadly. "That's what I thought. And the fact that you felt that way . . . made me take a good hard look at myself. Maybe I've been asking too much of you . . ."

"No," I protested. "I like helping!"

"I know you love cooking, but that's not what I'm talking about. I'm worried I sometimes put the business ahead of family." She sighed and looked me in the eye. "So, here's the deal. You are still in trouble for lying, so you're grounded for the next week. You'll come right home after school. No going to Nina's house. No phone. And no posts on Relay."

"Okay." No phone would suck, and I'd miss being able to post on my favorite social media site, but I'd live. I held my breath and waited to hear the rest.

"As far as these two," Mom said, nodding toward the pugs,

who were happily curled up by my feet. "We'll go around the neighborhood today and put up some more flyers."

"And if we don't find the owners?"

Mom's eyes narrowed. "One step at a time. They can stay here until we find the owners. If we don't find them—that's another conversation. Deal?"

I felt a little relieved. Just a little. "Deal."

Dad walked into the house then, carrying two big shopping bags. "Somebody order some kibble?" he asked with a wink at me.

"Oh my gosh, thank you!" I took one of the bags from him. "I didn't know what I was going to feed them this morning."

"I was just following orders," he told me with a nod in Mom's direction. Her head was down as she unpacked one of the bags.

I stared at Mom until she looked up. She shrugged. "Well, I just knew they weren't getting any more beef Wellington," she said with a smirk.

I smiled and bent down to pet the pugs as Dad handed me a pair of cereal bowls to put the kibble in. They were staying, at least for the time being.

Now I just had to hope that nobody came forward to claim them.

Just then, my little brother, Ollie, crashed in through the front door, back from his weekend at Colin's. He looked surly, probably because he hadn't slept well; he was often cranky when coming back from staying at a friend's.

Ollie seemed to sense the tension in the air because he looked at me and asked, "What'd I miss?"

The girl dog came over to him, stood on her hind legs, and since Ollie's pretty short, she put her paws almost up to his waist. His face changed and he asked again, this time in a completely different tone of voice, "Oh man, what did I miss?"

Mom looked surprised at the huge smile that spread across Ollie's face.

It *was* nice to see Ollie smile.

And also, score one point for Team Dog.

Mom had a three-pronged plan to find the pugs' owners. First, she had me go get the flyer I'd put up on the community bulletin board. She said the picture was good, but she typed out new text, using her cell phone number instead of mine. She made a horrified face at the thought that mine had been hanging up in our neighborhood for almost two days. "You're lucky you're already grounded," she told me.

Then, with more flyers printed, Mom, Dad, Ollie, and I went around to the neighbors' houses and knocked on some doors. The neighbor directly behind us, Mr. Porter, was first. He is notoriously grumpy, so he mostly just grunted and shook his head when we handed him a flyer. "Dogs are more trouble than they're worth," he said, and went back inside his house.

"Have a nice day," Dad called as Mr. Porter slammed his gate shut.

Some neighbors had locked gates, like our house, so we had to wait for someone to notice our feet under the gate. At a couple of houses no one came out, even though there were cars in their assigned spaces, so we slipped the flyers under the gate. One lady I didn't know seemed rather interested in the pugs, even though she didn't say they were hers.

"They're not very good dogs," Ollie told her. "I don't like them."

The lady looked confused, but Mom just asked her to keep an ear out for someone looking for missing dogs and told her to have a nice day.

"What was that?" Dad asked Ollie when her door closed.

"I want to keep them," Ollie said.

Dad's sympathetic face as he patted Ollie on the head made me add one more member to Team Dog.

We finished our neighborhood, visiting every town house where we could get someone to answer the door. We got no takers, and I felt a mix of relief and disappointment.

When we got home and fed the dogs (who were very happy to see us after being alone most of the afternoon), Mom revealed the third part of her plan. That was for me to put up a post about the dogs on Relay, and then she'd share the same post on Facebook. Mom said she'd suspend my online grounding so I could post, but she suggested I start a new account just to post the picture of the pugs. And she stayed with me while I made the post to be sure I wasn't using my own phone number this time. "I still can't believe you did that," she grumbled under her breath as I typed in her number.

I finished and hit POST. Then I pulled the boy dog, who was snuggled up beside me, into my lap and started scratching under his chin. He gave a happy groan and I laughed.

Mom gave me a look. "Sam, you should be careful about getting too attached. We just started looking. And after that . . ."

"I know," I broke in, putting my chin on top of the little dog's head. "I know," I repeated in a lower voice, mostly to myself.

When she walked away, I whispered to him, "Love you. Don't forget, okay?"

Mom was right that I shouldn't get too attached. But it was already too late.

5

The Pizzazz

"You did *what*?"

Nina had been leaning back in her chair in study hall but she sat up quickly, the front two legs of the chair hitting the tile floor with a loud *thwack*.

Our study hall proctor didn't even blink. She seemed to be watching something on her iPad. I loved the end of the year.

"After I texted you, I hid the dogs in my room for the rest of the night," I repeated calmly. It was weird updating Nina on something so long after the fact. I'd never lost phone privileges before. At least Mom had let me send Nina *one* text on Sunday to explain about my grounding. I'd told Mom that otherwise Nina might send the National Guard to our house looking for me. I wasn't sure what the National Guard was, but it was something adults said, and it sounded like the kind of thing Nina would do if she couldn't get in touch with me.

"That's so not you, Sam!" Nina whispered now. "I can't remember you being so sneaky, like, ever. Your mom must have completely freaked."

"Well, I am grounded. But she actually said the dogs could stay—at least while we look for their owners."

"Do you think you'll find them?"

I rearranged the pencils in my case as a distraction. "I don't know. I don't even know what to hope for. It feels selfish and kind of mean to hope we don't find them—since the chances of me being allowed to keep the dogs aren't even very good. Anyway, the whole thing's a long shot. We'll probably find the owners. I mean, the dogs probably just got . . . delivered to the wrong address."

Nina looked skeptical. "Sam, I hate to be the one to have to tell you this, but dogs don't get delivered, not even on Amazon

Prime. Somebody was dumping them off so they could get rid of them."

"You think so? But that's so sad!"

"My aunt Rachel in Michigan is a vet. She says people dump dogs and cats at their office all the time. Like, every week."

I frowned. "Who could do that? That's horrible!"

"People are horrible sometimes. But, Sam, whatever happens, I don't think it's wrong for you to want to keep them. They'd be lucky to get adopted by you. I for one am rooting for you. And I can't wait to meet them in real life. They were insanely cute in the pics you sent."

"They *are* insanely cute," I agreed. I felt a little bit better already, after sharing everything that had happened with Nina. Maybe she was right and it wasn't so wrong to hope.

I reached into my bag and pulled out my recipe book. I used it to jot down different ideas for recipes. What I kept in my backpack was my travel version. Once I'd perfected a recipe I'd type it out, print it, laminate it, and put it in my *real* recipe book.

It has been suggested to me by some people that this process is ridiculous, but not by Nina. She always wants everything to be perfect, too, so she gets it.

Nina leaned forward again. "So, what are you working on now? And when can I taste it?"

"Lemon tahini chicken. As for the second part, as soon as I'm not grounded anymore." I showed her the recipe. "I'm worried it's still missing . . . something."

"Let me guess. The pizzazz?" Nina smiled and rolled her eyes, but I knew she was only teasing. She understands my obsession with "the pizzazz"—which is what I always call that one special ingredient, the one twist that I put on every recipe that makes it unique. I firmly believe that the key to any recipe's success is the pizzazz.

"What were you thinking to use?" Nina asked.

"Black sesame seeds, but just as a garnish. Which is basically cheating."

"Why can't the pizzazz be the garnish?" Nina argued. "It's still part of the dish."

"I guess it could. I'm not sure it feels right, though."

"Go with your gut," Nina said, and I nodded. Even though my best friend is the world's greatest planner, the thing she's best at is something you can't plan at all: improvisational comedy. Our school has an improv team called the In-Betweeners and Nina is the captain. She's also the funniest one. She's been trying to get me to audition for the troupe for the past two years, but I'm more of a behind-the-scenes girl. I can't imagine getting up onstage and winging it like that. It definitely takes a kind of bravery that I just don't have. *Although*, said a little voice in my head, *you* did *just hide two dogs in your room for over twenty-four hours.*

When I got home from school, Ollie was sitting on the living room floor playing with the pugs.

"Nobody called about them?" I asked, putting down my backpack.

Ollie shook his head. "Nope. I think we should keep them." He threw something round and the pugs tumbled over each other to fetch it.

"What is that?" I asked him.

"A pair of socks."

I smiled. It seemed Ollie and I had the same idea for a "toy" to entertain the pugs. I wished Dad had picked up some doggy toys when he'd gone to pick up the food yesterday.

I sat down beside Ollie on the floor. "I'd like to keep them, but good luck convincing Mom and Dad. Mostly Mom," I added.

"I can help take care of them."

"That'd be great. Speaking of, have you taken them outside yet this afternoon?"

Ollie looked guilty. "I didn't think of it."

I stood up. "Well, if you want to help convince Mom and Dad, you're going to have to start thinking about that part. If one of them goes in the house, our campaign is over before it even starts."

"Okay, I'll remember. Hey, we should name them Groot and Rocket!" Ollie said excitedly.

"Whoa, Olls. First, if you look a little closer, you'll see *that* one is a girl. Second, if we do get to keep them, *I'm* the one who found them. I get to pick the names." I handed him one of the two harness-and-leash combos that Dad had bought when he got the food yesterday.

"No fair."

"Life isn't fair, Ollie. You also get to play video games while I help Mom."

"Yeah, but you *like* cooking."

"I like cooking. Folding three hundred wontons, like I have to do this afternoon, is a whole other story."

"Mom had me try to fold a few but they came out looking like garbage so she said I could go play."

I looked at my little brother. "Are you sure you didn't fold them like garbage on purpose?"

Ollie kept a straight face but I thought I saw the ghost of a triumphant smile. Ollie was a sweet kid, but he was also a master at tricking our parents. He even, occasionally, managed to trick me.

"Where is Mom?" I asked him. "I thought you said she had you trying to fold wontons but the van is gone."

"She had to go get something. Mirror something."

"Mirin, probably. It's a kind of rice wine used in Asian cooking."

Ollie shrugged. I opened the door for him to step through with the girl dog, who'd seemed to take a special liking to Ollie right away. I was rather partial to the boy myself, so I didn't really mind. But she stayed put, waiting for her brother, as usual, so I ended up walking out first anyway.

"Can't we name them, Sam?" Ollie begged me while we waited for the pugs to do their business. "*Please?*"

I felt myself weakening. It *was* getting ridiculous to think of the pugs as only "Boy" and "Girl." We could just give them names for now, I told myself. To use until we found the real owners, who no doubt had given the dogs other names.

"Okay," I said, feeling a spark of excitement. "I've actually been thinking about food names, of course."

"Of course," Ollie said with a smirk. "Like what?"

"I'm thinking a pair of names. Like Salt and Pepper," I said. The girl dog barked in our direction and her tail wagged. Had she liked those names?

Ollie frowned. "You can't call a dog Salt. That's a dumb name."

True. "Okay," I said. "I also thought of Mac and Cheese—but it's sort of the same problem. Cheese isn't that cute of a name. And it's also not a very sophisticated dish."

Ollie rolled his eyes. "How about Sugar and Spice?" he offered, which I had to admit wasn't bad. But it didn't quite *fit*.

"Hmm, maybe," I said. I picked up the boy dog and Ollie scooped up the girl and we headed back into the house.

"Bacon and Eggs?" Ollie suggested, and I shook my head. That was a definite *no*.

But as we put the pugs down on the blanket in the kitchen, inspiration hit me.

"I got it!" I cried, grinning. "Pepper and Jack! Like pepper jack cheese. You know, the kind I use for nachos?"

"Mmm," Ollie said. "I'm getting hungry."

"Pepper's cute for the girl," I added. "Like Pepper Potts in *Iron Man*. And Jack would be great for the boy. He seems like a Jack, doesn't he?"

The girl dog barked again, and I remembered how I'd suggested Pepper earlier. She must have liked *that* name! And soon her brother—Jack, as I was already thinking of him—joined her.

Their barks sounded happy. They had to be Pepper and Jack! I just hoped Ollie would agree.

"I like it," Ollie said with a grin, and I couldn't help it—I pulled him into a big hug. He let me hug him for a second before he pushed me away with an annoyed groan.

Mom came into the kitchen then, carrying a bunch of plastic grocery bags. I knew she was in a hurry since she hadn't even taken her reusable canvas bags. She was usually the person at the store who gave everyone a dirty look for ruining the planet with plastic bags.

"So, we ran out of mirin?" I asked, taking a few bags from her.

"How did you know?" Mom asked with a smile. "Don't tell me Ollie remembered what I said."

"Nope, he called it *mirror*, but I figured it out."

"I should have realized you would."

Mom opened the cabinets to put the groceries away. "So," she added, "I did some searching online for the best shelter, in case we need it. It looks like a place called Rescue Buddies has the best reviews."

I looked down at Pepper and Jack. They had snuggled up

close together with Pepper's head resting on Jack's back. I felt something inside my heart snap.

I couldn't imagine taking them to a shelter. Abandoning them there just like all those people who left sweet dogs and cats on the doorstep of Nina's aunt's vet office? Just like they'd been abandoned on our porch. What if they got separated—or worse, what if no one adopted them? I couldn't bear the thought of what could happen next.

"No!" I said, the word bursting out of me at a louder volume than I'd planned.

Mom turned to face me. "What do you mean, *no*?"

She sounded genuinely surprised, and why wouldn't she? I was always the good daughter, the one who helped out without really complaining. The one she could leave a to-do list for, knowing that everything on it would get done, and done well. My brother's lists, on the other hand, were really just for show— so it seemed like we were being treated equally. I was always helpful. So I deserved this one thing, just this one time.

I took a deep breath. "I mean, no—we can't take them to a shelter. I won't . . . we just can't."

"Sam, I know it's not a fun thing to have to do. But we had a deal."

"The deal was that we would see if we could find the owners and *then* figure out what to do! But you're already jumping ahead to dumping them at a shelter! Please, Mom—I've never asked you for anything like this, but I'm asking now." I looked down at their tiny, sweet faces. "If we can't find the owners, I want to keep them. So . . . we can't take them to a shelter."

Mom was already shaking her head. "Sam, you know we're gone too much. It wouldn't be fair to them . . ."

"We're only gone at night—you and Dad work from home most days!" I argued.

"This is not open for debate." Mom started unpacking the grocery bags.

"I'm not debating. I'm negotiating! If you want me to keep helping you with the business, then you'll give me this."

Mom put the bottle of mirin down slowly on the counter and looked up at me. I knew instantly that she was mad—worse even than when the dogs had gotten loose at the Wilkerson party.

"You know you need me!" I pressed on, feeling reckless now. "I'm a good chef—who are you going to rely on for help if not me? Oliver? Maybe you can offer a spray-cheese special!" I didn't even really know what I was saying. I was just trying to fill the angry silence. My face felt hot. I was angry and embarrassed and worried all at the same time. But still, when I thought of having to take the pugs to a shelter, I couldn't bring myself to give up.

"You need me!" I repeated. "I bring the pizzazz!" I added in desperation. Just then, Dad walked in the door.

He looked from Mom to me, then down at Ollie. "Is everything okay?"

"Sam and Mom are fighting," he said.

"What are you grinning about?" Dad asked him.

"I think I'm gonna enjoy being the favorite kid," Ollie replied.

6

Pepper and Jack (Don't)
Join the Party

That night, I skipped dinner, which was a first for me. I went to
bed with an empty stomach that still felt sick, but not from hunger. I'd never rebelled against my parents this way. I was pretty
sure that I'd feel better if I went downstairs, apologized, and said
that I understood why the pups had to go to a shelter. But I'd
brought Pepper and Jack to my room with me (under strict orders
to keep them quiet and clean up any messes) and one look into
their big, trusting eyes and I couldn't make my feet walk
down the stairs.

So I waited until everyone went to bed to take Pepper and Jack outside. Except I'd miscalculated and Dad was still up watching TV.

"Hey, kiddo," he said, and I squeaked in surprise, almost dropping an armful of pugs. "It's okay," Dad added. "I'm not mad at you. In fact, I wanted to check on you."

I sighed and sat down on the sofa, putting the pugs beside me.

"You have to understand your mom," Dad said. "She really doesn't want to adopt two dogs."

"What about you?" I asked.

"I actually think it could be good for you and your brother to have pets." I opened my mouth to say I agreed, but Dad raised a hand. "Before you get too excited, any decision like that has to be approved by both of us. *Especially* your mother," he added with a wink. "But I did convince her to take some more time to consider. I told her that you must feel strongly about these little ones for you to resort to threatening not to help out with the food prep anymore."

I stroked Pepper's back and her tail wagged. "I do. I mean,

when I first found them, I was really only thinking about how we could find the owners. But now . . ."

"I get it. They are pretty cute."

"So . . . how much longer am I grounded for?" I held my breath.

"Your mother didn't mention it. But you'd better be the perfect kid from now until the end of your original grounding. *And* get those two off the couch and take them outside."

"Okay. I will. On both counts." I turned back around. "Thanks, Dad."

He nodded and smiled and looked back at the TV.

The week passed with things still tense between Mom and me. That weekend, we had another event: Sarah Metzger's bat mitzvah at the Crescent Hotel. Sarah was in my grade, and I'd actually been invited to the party as a guest. But I wanted to make things right with Mom, so I said I'd be happy to help out with the catering. And Mom and Dad agreed I should have time off to go hang out with my friends during the party, too.

The one catch? I had to wear my black-and-white waitress uniform.

Of course, the whole thing was complicated by the fact that I had to bring the pugs along with me to the event. Ollie was at Colin's house again (conveniently), so they would have been alone at home. The dogs seemed to be pretty young—during the day they needed to go outside every couple of hours, and the event would take six hours, at least. With the cleanup, it could take longer.

I'd found an extra plastic laundry basket in our storage closet, and lined the bottom with fresh towels. Now, just outside the kitchen of the Crescent Ballroom, I set Pepper and Jack into the basket, put a plastic bowl for water into the corner of the basket, and went to join the party.

Nina came over to find me. She was there with a couple of girls from our school, Allie and Ana.

"Where are these adorable pugs?" Nina cried as soon as she saw me.

"Follow me," I said. Luckily, Mom and Dad and their servers were setting up buffet tables in the ballroom. I led Nina,

Allie, and Ana over to where I'd put the laundry basket. "Meet Pepper and Jack," I announced.

"Ooh, they're so cute!" Nina exclaimed. She knelt down to hug Pepper, who promptly licked her cheek. Allie petted Jack, who thumped his tail against the side of the basket.

"I love their little wrinkly faces," Ana said. "My cousin Matt has a pug."

"Yeah, they're pretty darn cute," I agreed. "I didn't mean to fall in love with them, but then, *poof*." I started to feel sad and decided a change of subject was in order. "I love your dresses," I said to Nina, Allie, and Ana.

"Thanks!" Allie cooed. "Cute waitress outfit."

"Thanks," I said, somewhat less enthusiastically. "I saw it and just *had* to have it."

When Nina, Allie, Ana, and I went back to the ballroom, the entertainment had started. Dr. Jams and his band were there, along with Jai. This time, Jai was singing lead vocals on all the songs, with his dad backing him up. And he was really, really good.

So good that all the other girls at the party had gathered in front of the stage like fans at a rock concert.

Nina grabbed my arm excitedly. "Can you believe this singer? He's amazing—and so cute! He looks just like Dev Patel—from that movie *Lion*!"

I looked up at Jai. "I mean, kind of . . ."

"Come on, Sam. Get your head out of your recipe book for a minute. He's gorgeous." Nina's blue eyes sparkled. "I'm telling my mom I don't want a DJ for my bat mitzvah! I want Dr. Jams!"

"First of all, my recipe book is not in my head. I mean, reverse that. Anyway, second, Jai is very talented . . ."

"His name is Jai? You mean you *know* him? You have to introduce us!"

"Does he go to our school?" Allie asked. "Or is he older?"

I shook my head. "He's our age but he lives in Maryland with his mom—he's just staying with his dad for the summer."

Then Jai started singing a Panic! At The Disco song. I turned to Nina and we screamed in excitement. We started jumping up and down in time to the music. I looked down at my cater-waiter clothes and felt jealous of the other girls' pretty party dresses, but Jai was such a great singer—and performer—that I pushed the feeling away and just enjoyed the music.

"What's his name again?" Nina asked me after the band had finished the song and walked off the stage for a break.

"Jai," said a voice behind me, and I jumped. I turned around, my heart racing, to find Jai standing there. "Hey, Sam," he said with a smile.

"Um, hi," I said, smiling back. Nina elbowed me in the ribs, and I remembered she wanted an introduction. "This is Nina—she's my best friend. And this is Ana and Allie."

"I'm Allie and she's Ana," Allie corrected me, and I felt my face turn red.

"Nice to meet you guys," Jai said. "Are you enjoying the party?"

"We *so* are. You're a really great singer!" Allie gushed.

"You should see me dance," Jai told her, and she turned pink and giggled. It was hard to believe that Jai was the same age as the boys in our class. How had he learned to be so confident? Just from performing onstage with his father? But then I realized that I'd been seeing Dr. J around the event circuit since well before last summer. Jai hadn't been around then. I wondered why he was here visiting his dad now, when he hadn't come in previous years.

The next thing I knew, Nina was snapping her fingers in front of my face. I blinked twice in surprise. I must have gone into a little trance pondering the mystery that was Jai. "Did you fall asleep standing up?" Nina asked.

"Catering's hard work," I mumbled.

"Speaking of, Sam and I'd better get back to work and let you all get back to the party," Jai told Nina, Allie, and Ana. I waved to the girls and followed Jai toward the kitchen.

"What work do *you* have to do in the kitchen?" I asked him.

"It just seemed like maybe you needed a small rescue."

I'm pretty sure I was beaming at him when my mom walked back to the kitchen and asked me to start putting the dessert on trays.

"This is Jai—he's Dr. Jams's son," I told her. "Jai, this is my mom."

"It's nice to meet you, Mrs. Calloway." Jai held out a hand to her.

"Nice to meet you, too," she said, smiling, no doubt at Jai's infectious charm. Then she went back out to help Dad carry the big cake.

"Oh, I brought you something." Jai handed me a small bag of dog treats. "These will probably help if you're trying to get them to cooperate. Pugs are very food-motivated."

"Dogs after my own heart. And thank you. I don't really know what I'm doing."

"You'll learn as you go."

I didn't have the heart just then to explain to Jai that I probably wouldn't get that chance. I walked over to the pugs in their laundry basket, and they barked when they saw Jai and me.

"I named them," I told Jai, giving them each a scratch behind the ears. "Meet Pepper and Jack."

"Great names," Jai told me with a grin.

I felt my face get warm, and I gave Pepper and Jack each one treat from the bag Jai had given me. The dogs were delighted. While they ate, I washed my hands and pulled a box of mochi out of its dry ice.

"Do you need help with that?" Jai pointed to the mochi.

71

"No, it's okay. Don't you have to go back on soon anyway?"

"Dad's going to do a couple of slow songs next. I can hang out."

"Okay," I said, feeling glad.

"What are these things, by the way?" Jai asked, coming closer.

"It's called mochi," I told him. "They're Japanese. Sticky rice with an ice cream filling. My dad made them." I noticed for the first time that he'd drawn little smiley faces on them with black icing. "Do you want to try one? I like the green ones—they're green-tea flavor."

"Sure—hit me with a green one." He popped the whole thing into his mouth and chewed thoughtfully. "I kind of like it."

Jai helped me put mochi balls on little plates. When we were done, Jai picked up Pepper from the basket and held up a leftover smiley pink mochi ball beside her head. "Hold on, that's too cute—I have to take a pic." Jai pulled his phone out of his pocket and snapped the pic. I felt a pang, missing my phone.

Finally, one of the band members came to get Jai. "The bat mitzvah girl keeps asking for you," the drummer said with an exaggerated wink at both of us.

"Thanks for the ice cream ball," Jai told me, putting Pepper back in the basket.

"No, thank you for helping me," I said. It had been really nice spending time with Jai.

After Jai had left, I picked up the finished dessert tray, ready to supply happy ice cream balls to the guests. But I knew for sure that none of them would look as cute as Jai had while eating them.

7

#pugtwins

On Sunday morning I woke up excited but nervous. My grounding was over, but I was still kind of afraid to ask for my phone back. After all, I'd definitely risked further grounding by accidentally threatening to stop helping my mom with events if she said we had to take the pugs to a shelter.

But when I went downstairs, my phone was sitting at my usual place at the kitchen table. Whew.

After taking Pepper and Jack outside to do their business, I brought the pugs and my phone upstairs and texted Nina good morning. I knew she was still sleeping in, so I sat on my bed and opened my laptop to log in to Relay.

First, I checked to see if the pug post I'd put up last week had any comments. A couple people had shared it—Nina, and a girl from school who was a grade below me. The post had one hundred and five views and six thumbs-ups, but no comments.

While I was logged on, I saw that Jai had found my username and tagged me in a photo. He'd posted the adorable picture of him with Pepper and the pink mochi ball.

I saw that Allie had reposted the pic, and she was basically a Relay celebrity—she had over three thousand followers! Only teen singers and actors had more followers than that.

Relay had started out as a social media site just for kids—unlike, say, Instagram. But according to Nina, some older people had started to get accounts. She predicted that in a few years it might be like Facebook, with everybody's parents and grandparents logging on. I hoped not—I loved Relay. It was definitely the home of the most creative hashtags. My personal best was #donutmissthisrecipe for my cinnamon walnut baked donuts.

Oh, the cute hashtags I could create for the pugs! But I was getting ahead of myself again.

Allie had added a super cute hashtag, though: #pugtwinsWPB—Pug Twins West Palm Beach. The pups weren't exactly twins, but it sure was catchy. I clicked through some of Allie's other photos, and then I couldn't resist clicking over to Jai's profile.

His profile picture was a great one of him performing onstage, maybe even from this summer. I read the rest of his profile:

Name: Jai Jambagi

5 Words That Describe Your Personality: Plus, Extra, Music, Food, Sunshine

#1 Skill: singing+dancing

#1 Jam: "Gallan Tipsiyaan"—Arjun Kanungo

#1 Best Friend: Dipper 🐾

#1 Place: Atlantic Ocean, esp. Ocean City

#1 Dream: perform 4 thousands!!!

I felt a flush of excitement. One of his top five words he used to describe himself was *food*! Of course, the rest of his number ones were mostly about singing, dancing, and performing— completely the opposite of behind-the-scenes me.

But his number-one best friend was his dog, which I had to respect.

I heard the Relay notification ding and realized it was another like for the pug-plus-Jai-plus-mochi post that I was tagged in. I couldn't believe it: Only a few minutes had passed, and the post already had eighty likes. I guessed I should be grateful for Allie's Relay celebrity.

Then my phone chimed with a text from Nina.

THANK GOODNESS YOU ARE FINALLY BACK ON THIS WAS TORTURE DON'T GET GROUNDED AGAIN.

I grinned. It really was good to be back.

Later that afternoon, Nina came over.

"Did you see Jai's Relay post?" she demanded as soon as I opened the front door for her. "Crazy how many likes it got, huh?"

"I did, and yeah, crazy! How does Allie have so many followers anyway?" I asked as we headed upstairs to my room. My parents were out grocery shopping, and Ollie was playing video games in his room. The pugs were napping on their blanket in my room.

"Her stepbrother's a photographer, and she's way into shopping," Nina explained, "so she posts really good pics of herself wearing all kinds of cool new stuff. Sometimes she gets freebies sent to her now. Last month a sunglasses company sent her a box of free pairs and asked her to tag their company."

"Seriously? I thought Relay was just for fun?"

"I think it started that way, but companies want our money, yo."

I laughed. "I guess so."

In my room, Nina sat down on the floor with the pugs while I flopped down on my bed. Pepper opened one eye, and then Jack opened one eye, and soon they were both awake and wagging their tails at Nina, who loved it.

"Listen, Sam," Nina said after a moment of playing with the pugs. "Allie actually texted me to get me to find out if Jai is dating anybody. She has a crush on him."

I glanced over at Nina. "What? Why? I mean, she just met him."

"I said she had a crush, not that she wanted to get engaged. Calm down. Unless . . ." Nina grinned. "You *like* him! I can't believe I didn't see it before. This explains that weird trance thing at the bat mitzvah!"

My cheeks were hot. "I'm not . . . I didn't . . . what do you mean *trance*?"

Nina's grin widened. "This is so interesting. Apparently, you can't talk when you've got a crush. Who would have guessed?"

"I can talk just fine, thank you very much. And I don't have a *crush*. He's just . . . nice."

"And cute."

"Yes," I admitted, feeling my stomach flip over. "*But* I don't have a crush. He doesn't even live here. It'll just be nice to have someone my own age around at the events this summer. Playing Uno with Ollie in the kitchen gets old after a while."

"Ollie puts down his Nintendo 2DS long enough to play cards with you?"

"I have to hide it first," I answered.

Nina giggled and took out her phone. She snapped a picture of the pugs frolicking on my rug. A few minutes later I heard a ding on my computer. I clicked on the notification and saw Nina had put up a new post on Relay.

It was a particularly cute pic of the two dogs. She'd used a filter to add cheese hats to each pug's head and typed the caption: Meet #pugtwinsWPB Pepper and Jack! They love to #saycheese for the camera!! #puglife #wpb #pugsofRelay.

"Aww, that's awesome," I said, turning to her.

"I aim to please," Nina said.

I heard yet another ding and gasped when I saw that I had one new friend request: from Jai Jambagi.

Clicking ACCEPT, I had to grin. I'd been thinking about sending him a request, but this was so much better.

"Hey! The pugs' cheese post already has over twenty likes! They're getting Relay famous for reals!" Nina announced, studying her phone.

"*Almost* as famous as Allie," I laughed, and Pepper barked, as if agreeing.

8

Shrimp Sam

On Friday afternoon, I walked with Nina down the hallway. The school year was officially over, and the hall was loud with kids talking excitedly about summer vacation.

"HAGS!" a boy from my PE class yelled to Nina and me, and then ran off yelling the same thing in everybody else's faces. I was pretty sure he didn't really care that I *Have A Great Summer.* Some of the boys in our grade had decided it was hilarious when shouted at close range.

To add to the noise, the principal's secretary was blasting an almost-unintelligible song over the PA system. The only word from the lyrics I could make out was *summer*.

"I can't believe it's finally summer," Nina said.

"Me neither. The last week seemed to take forever." It was true. It had been an endless parade of class parties, junk food, and of course, semi-educational movies. But every afternoon, I'd rushed home to hang out with Pepper and Jack.

Even though summer was always busy for Calloway's Creations, I was looking forward to more time in the kitchen and less time behind a desk struggling through math problems or science labs. Unlike Nina, I wasn't good at every subject, so my final report card would probably be just as lopsided as usual, with As in language arts and social studies but Bs in everything else.

As long as I could get into a good culinary school, though, that was all I cared about. I'd known I wanted to be a chef for as long as I could remember. So more time to spend concocting recipes was good in my book.

I was also starting to dare to hope that I'd have even more

time to spend with Pepper and Jack. But there were still two big obstacles: they probably belonged to somebody else (even though no one had come forward yet), and if not, Mom would still have to say yes to our keeping them.

But soon we'd all have a big distraction. Tomorrow was one of Calloway's Creations's biggest events of the summer: the Danvers' wedding.

The wedding was being held at a very fancy venue on Palm Beach Island, and my parents had hired a bunch of extra servers to help. My aunt Maddie was even coming down from Orlando to help us get the food ready.

Mom and Dad were so serious about the Danvers' wedding that they had arranged for Ollie to stay overnight at Colin's house again so he wouldn't be underfoot. Mom had even called Colin's parents to ask about the pups coming with Ollie, but it turned out that Mr. Givens, Colin's dad, was allergic.

I filled Nina in on this news as we walked home together. Then I gave her a big hug and we said goodbye; she'd be leaving for California early the next morning.

"I'll text you," she promised, giving me an extra hug. "Later, frieeennnd."

"Later!" I called, and then turned to hurry home.

My aunt's car was parked in the driveway, so I ran into the house, excited to see her. But first I looked down for Pepper and Jack, who always greeted me with an enthusiastic attack on my lower legs. Then I heard rattling and looked over to see that they were both tumbling around in a blue crate.

"What's this?" I asked Mom, who was coming into the living room from the kitchen.

"It's a travel crate," Mom explained. "So we can bring them to the wedding tomorrow," she added reluctantly. "Your father borrowed it from his friend Doug."

I nodded. The pugs *were* getting too big for the laundry crate that we'd used at the last event, and this blue crate looked nice and roomy.

"Do they need to be in it now?" I asked Mom.

"I prefer them to be in it when you're not home," Mom replied. "Just so they're more under control. I looked it up online and apparently crate training is the way to go." She paused, then added, "But enough about dogs. How was your last day of school, hon?"

"It was good." I frowned, distracted, and glanced back down at the pugs in their crate. "Can I let them out?"

Mom nodded. "Yes."

I opened the crate, and then I had to crouch down and give each pug a hug . . . then scratch their bellies, since they both promptly rolled over onto their backs. Jack wouldn't roll over again, so I kept on scratching. He's absolutely insatiable when it comes to belly scratches.

"Hi, Sammy! Nice to see you, too."

I heard my aunt's familiar voice and I looked up to see Maddie standing over me with her hands on her hips. She was nearly covered in flour—it was in her hair and I even spotted some on her shoes. She must have been standing there for some time while I played with the pugs.

I stood up. Maddie's messy look was in contrast to her sister, my mother, who looked perfect as usual. I had to smile. Maybe I'd inherited the messy-cook gene from my aunt.

"Sorry, Maddie. They're just soooo cute." I went to hug my aunt but she gestured to the flour on the front of her apron and blew me a kiss instead. "I missed you," I added, blowing a kiss back. "Feels like it's been forever."

"Missed you, too. Seems like there have been some new developments around here." Maddie looked pointedly at the two pugs, who were still playing around my feet.

"Nothing permanent yet," Mom put in.

I was sure my aunt didn't miss the frown that crossed my face at that comment. "I thought you were coming tomorrow," I told Aunt Maddie.

"I talked to your mother and I could tell she was in panic mode, so I got in the car and drove down early."

"What would I do without my little sister?" Mom asked, giving Maddie a side hug in spite of the flour.

"I wonder if I'll ever be able to say something similar about *my* younger sibling?" I mused out loud. I could hear Ollie playing video games up in his room. Maddie laughed.

Mom shook her head. "Of *course* you will. Someday."

"Especially if you ever need help playing video games or not taking out the trash," Maddie added, and Mom threw a dishrag at her, sending puffs of flour into the air. They headed back into the kitchen together, cracking up.

I was glad Maddie was here. Mom always seemed younger and happier with her around. I wished my aunt didn't live three hours away, but she works for a theme park, and she loves her job. So I knew she wasn't moving back down to West Palm Beach anytime soon.

Just then, I thought of Jai, and how his home was really far away, in Maryland. I realized I hadn't even asked him where specifically he lived. Although I had no reason to go to Maryland; I'd never been anywhere farther north than Atlanta.

"Earth to Sam." Maddie's voice broke into my thoughts again. My aunt was peeking out of the kitchen.

"Sorry. What'd you say?"

"I was asking about the menu for this wedding. Your mom said you came up with a new appetizer that you were going to make?"

I nodded enthusiastically and hurried into the kitchen. "I'm sure Mom told you the theme for the food is like a twist on elegant Southern cooking? My recipe is an update on shrimp and grits, but as a handheld appetizer—with a corn bread crust. The pizzazz is a fried sage leaf on top." I could use my shorthand with Aunt Maddie—she knew all about my need for pizzazz in recipes.

"Yum!" Maddie turned to Mom. "Hey, Melissa, I think your daughter should make a batch tonight—you know, so we can test them out."

"Nice try, sis. She already made a batch last week. And we can't afford any more practice shrimp."

"No problem!" Maddie pulled off her apron with a flourish, sending even more flour into the air as Mom frowned. "You've been making last-minute lists all day—Sam and I will go get everything, and I'll pick up some shrimp. My treat."

Mom sighed. "Okay, twist my arm. But first Sam has something she has to take care of."

Mom was staring at me and it took a couple of seconds to shift gears in my brain away from thoughts of cooking. "Oh!

Right, I—just have to feed Pepper and Jack and take them out-side first."

"Pepper and Jack?" Maddie asked.

"The pugs. I named them," I explained, a little sheepishly. "Just for the time they're with us. What do you think?"

"Adorable!" Aunt Maddie said, and I gave her a hug. It was nice to have someone visiting who really got me.

Mom frowned once more, but I tried to ignore it as I got out the dogs' food.

The next day, we started packing up the van before noon. Pepper and Jack seemed excited to be going somewhere again. I guess they were already used to traveling all around, even as young as they were. In honor of the Danvers' wedding, I'd broken into Mom's gift-wrapping station and found one pink and one blue satin ribbon, and given each dog a bow tie. Then I snapped pic-tures of Pepper and Jack in their finery and posted a photo to Relay before climbing into the van with Mom, Dad, and Maddie.

As Dad pulled the catering van into a parking space, I imme-diately spotted Dr. Jams's van with its familiar stencil: a silhouette of him standing onstage holding a mic. I wondered if Jai would be performing.

I didn't have to wonder long, since when we entered the ballroom, he was up onstage doing the mic check.

I walked over to him. "You guys are here early."

"Hi," Jai said. "Yeah, my dad said this venue's not one of his usual spots, so he wanted to do a run-through of everything and then we could go get a late lunch. Do you want to come with us? We're going someplace to get seafood, that's all I know."

"I wish I could, but speaking of seafood, I have three hundred shrimp to prepare."

Jai raised his eyebrows. "Is this a Sam-original recipe?"

"It is!" I said proudly. "This will be the public debut of—well, I don't have a name for it yet."

"Describe it. Maybe I can help think of a name."

I laughed. "It's a shrimp and cheese grits appetizer on a corn bread crust. There's a dab of thyme butter sauce, a sprinkle of crispy bacon pieces, and a fried sage leaf on top."

"My mouth is watering, but I can't think of anything except Shrimp Sam."

I tilted my head to one side. "Hmm. That sounds like a nickname for me, 'cause I'm short!"

Jai's eyes were sparkling. "That wasn't intentional." He paused, thinking. "Sam's Shrimp, then? I just hope there are leftovers."

"Don't worry. I'll save you a couple."

Jai smiled. "Okay, well, I'll see you later. Maybe when you're on a break."

"I can take one whenever—you're the one who has to *break* it to your adoring fans that you're leaving the stage."

"Wow, that was a really terrible pun. Okay, I'll come find you on my break from my *adoring* fans." He waved and headed across the stage to where his dad and the other band members were setting up. I looked at my watch. It was time to get cracking on Shrimp Sam.

First, I took Jack and then Pepper out to a secluded patch of grass to do their business. Then I gave them each a treat and settled them back in their travel crate in a remote corner near the kitchen.

Mom was shaking her head when I turned back around.

"What?" I asked her. "What did I forget to do?"

"Nothing I can see. You're doing a good job with them, not that I should be surprised. I was just thinking that the fact that we're having *dogs* at events probably shouldn't go in our brochure."

"Do you think it's okay, though?" I asked, feeling a stab of worry.

Mom laughed. "Since they're too young to stay home alone for such a long stretch, we're just gonna go with it."

"Wow, Mom, I've never known you to be so rebellious."

"You have no idea," Aunt Maddie said, coming up behind Mom and slinging one arm around her. "The stories I could tell."

Mom glared at her. "But you won't, since you respect and appreciate your older sister so very much."

"Are you sure about that?" Maddie asked, and Mom swatted her on the behind before heading back to work. I went in search of the shrimp we'd brought and started assembling the other ingredients for my dish.

Soon, the time was passing lightning fast. That often happens when I'm cooking. It's not that I'm not thinking—actually

I'm concentrating very hard. But it's different than working on something at school. While I'm cooking I feel really relaxed, because everything else in the world just goes away. I wasn't worrying about what would happen with Pepper and Jack, or worrying about next year at school, or wishing Nina would get back from her trip already—I was just cooking. It was my happy place.

Before I knew it, I was plating my dish, and changing into my catering clothes so that I could take a tray around. Since Mom and Dad had hired extra help for the wedding, I didn't actually *have* to carry trays, but I wanted to be there for the debut of Shrimp Sam.

Guests in fancy dresses and suits were milling around, sipping glasses of champagne. The bride in her white gown and the groom in his tuxedo were in the midst of the crowd, hugging and kissing everyone. I walked my tray over to a family in the corner: a mom, a dad, and a teenage boy who was pulling at his collar and clearly counting the minutes until he could get out of the suit he wore. Each adult took one shrimp, and the boy started to say no, but then changed his mind and took one. The parents seemed to enjoy the food, but didn't say anything. I turned to head to the next group of people, but then the teenager patted me on the arm and grabbed two more Shrimp Sams. "Those are amazing!" he said, his mouth full. "I could eat twelve."

"You are not eating *twelve* appetizers," his mother chastised. "Those are for everyone. But . . . you're right. I will have one more," she said, and took another for herself while giving me a wink.

I felt like I imagined Jai must feel when everyone was clapping for him at the end of a song. It didn't really matter that they didn't know I'd made the food—all that mattered was that they found it really delicious. I floated happily around the room, offering the shrimp to more guests.

My dream of being a chef felt closer just then, even though I knew it was still years away. I couldn't wait to have that feeling in my own restaurant someday.

After my tray was empty, I went to check on the pugs. I knelt down and they tumbled forward in their crate, ecstatic to see me. At that moment I added a note to my recurring dream for the future. When I grew up, I'd have a restaurant with an outdoor seating area that was dog-friendly.

I gave them each a treat, then whispered in each of their ears. "Love you. Don't forget."

They looked back at me with their round, dark eyes, their way of saying the exact same thing.

9

Like a Barnacle

The best part about working an event is cleaning up afterward. It's not that I love to clean or anything. But at some venues, after all the guests leave, we get to spend time with the staff and the band or DJ. We share leftover food, someone plays music, and everyone's tired but usually in a good mood since the dealing-with-people part of the event is over. Sometimes guests can start to put us in a bad mood with rude behavior or outlandish requests, but as soon as all the paying customers are gone, those frustrations turn into funny stories, and the person who's had the worst run-in can usually get the most laughs.

Tonight had become one of those nights for me. When I'd come back out with another tray of Shrimp Sam, one lady in a very fancy dress had crammed an entire appetizer in her mouth *before* asking me (with her mouth still full) if it contained seafood.

"I mean, there's an *entire* shrimp sitting right there. Has the woman never seen a shrimp before? And then she's all, 'I simply cannot consume shellfish.'" I paused for dramatic effect and an eye roll. Everyone around me laughed, and I stroked Jack's ear as he lay beside me. Pepper was being a traitor and was curled up in Jai's lap, snoring.

Jai and I were sitting on the edge of the stage, and my parents, Maddie, and Dr. Jams were sitting at what had been the head table at the wedding a couple of hours ago.

"Did she end up having an allergic reaction?" Aunt Maddie asked.

I shook my head. "No. And later I saw her eating a big hunk of Mom's crawfish pie. So either she's confused about what a shellfish is, or . . ."

"She just enjoys being difficult," Dr. Jams put in.

Jai smiled. "Shrimp Sam is so good, I'd eat it even if I did have a shellfish allergy."

He'd just eaten the appetizers I'd stashed away for him and licked his fingers to demonstrate how much he'd liked them. I smiled back at him, feeling grateful and a little shy.

"When people have that allergy, their airway usually closes up, making it hard to, you know, breathe. So you might want to rethink that," Maddie told him.

Jai nodded. "Yikes. That's nothing to joke about. Are you a nurse?" he asked.

"No, but I work in customer service. We try to prevent people's airways from closing up since that tends to put a damper on the theme park experience."

Jai laughed. "That makes sense. Thanks for saving me some shrimp, Sam."

"You're welcome," I laughed. "By the way, I decided that is the name. Shrimp Sam."

He cocked his head to the side. "You *are* pretty short, so it works."

I laughed and pretended to kick him.

Maddie and my parents got up then to finish putting some stuff away, and Dr. Jams went over to help them, so it was just Jai and me.

"Hey, so I sent you a DR on Relay yesterday, but you never wrote back," Jai said.

I felt my cheeks turn pink. Jai had sent me a message? "I was super busy prepping for this wedding," I explained. "I didn't get a chance to check Relay."

"I get it," Jai said. "I do enjoy the pics you post of these guys."

I looked down at Jack's sleeping face and couldn't resist scratching the little space between his eyes, where the fur was so, so soft. "Your dog is adorable, too," I told Jai, even though saying so gave away the fact that I had scrolled through his profile.

But Jai only nodded with a smile. "I miss Dipper so much. I can't believe I won't see him for more than a month still. At first my mom was sending me pictures every day but she's slowed down now, and I feel bad bugging her. She's having to take him out and do everything for him since I'm not there."

"Do you always visit your dad in the summer?"

Jai looked uncomfortable suddenly, and I regretted asking the question. But he answered. "Not always." I didn't ask anything else.

I could see my parents heading out of the ballroom, and Aunt Maddie waved to me. It seemed that the after-party was over, so I stood to go. I picked up Jack, and without me having to ask, Jai picked up Pepper and carried her over to the travel crate for me.

"Thanks," I said as Jai helped me put the pugs back inside their crate.

Jai nodded. "Sure. I guess I'll see you at the next event," he said. "And online," he added with a wink.

The next day started with my aunt teasing me about Jai, or as she called him: "that singer boy you have a crush on." I quickly closed the Relay window where I'd been composing a message to send to Jai. Jack, whose head had been in my lap, looked at me in annoyance that I had moved and disturbed his nap.

"I don't have a crush!" I protested. I glanced around the living room, feeling my cheeks turn pink. Thankfully, my parents had gone out to brunch, so Maddie was staying with Ollie and me. And Ollie was playing his handheld game and wearing his giant noise-canceling headphones, so he hadn't heard anything. Adorably, Pepper's head was resting on Ollie's leg.

I tilted my head meaningfully in my little brother's direction. If Ollie *did* hear something, I'd be in trouble. Ollie tended to have a big mouth; I'd be mortified if he opened it and said something embarrassing in front of Jai at the next event.

Maddie gave me a knowing smile. "Maybe it's not a crush yet, but mark my words: It soon will be. I think you like him. And it's pretty clear he likes you, too."

"Maddie!" I yelled, and then Ollie did take off his headphones. Now it was Pepper's turn to look annoyed at *his* sudden movement.

"What's going on? Is the pizza here?"

"Oliver, it's ten thirty in the morning," I told him.

"You promised pizza," he said to our aunt.

"Yes. At lunchtime." She turned to me. "Should we be worried about this kid?"

"I think definitely yes," I said.

Ollie stuck his tongue out at me and then put his headphones back on, but I saw him scratch Pepper's chin before diving back into his game.

"I know we were sort of kidding, but I *am* kind of worried about Ollie," Maddie said in a quieter tone. "I feel like he gets left out a lot."

"He could totally be involved; he just doesn't want to *do* anything. If Mom and Dad ask him to load the dishwasher, he throws the plates and glasses in there like a lunatic. The other week, Mom tried to get him to roll up wontons with her, and he folded them into giant smushes."

Maddie frowned. "Cooking's not his thing. Or kitchen-related work," she added when I opened my mouth to say that loading a dishwasher wasn't exactly a culinary challenge. "But since that's the glue of this family, he gets left out a lot."

"That's true," I said thoughtfully. I looked back down at my laptop; I'd heard a notification ding.

"Thank you," Maddie said. "At work, I'm rather known for my insight. Hey! What's so interesting on your laptop there, kettle?"

"Kettle?"

"As in pot calling one black. And you're still not paying attention to me."

"I'm sorry, I just . . . I can't believe this post! It's already got fifty likes!"

"Your post?" Maddie came to peer over my shoulder.

"Jai posted it, but he tagged me." I showed her the picture. Jai had taken it last night; it was before Pepper's pink bow had come untied and before Jack started to snack on his blue bow tie. Jai had been wearing a tux for the wedding, and he'd held up one pug on either side of his face so that their three bow ties were all lined up in a row. It was adorable, so I quickly reposted it to the pugs' Relay page, and used the hashtag #pugtwinsWPB.

"Pretty cute," Maddie said. "Don't you think?"

"Very!" I said.

"And the pugs, too?" Maddie asked, nudging me with a laugh.

"Ugh!" I narrowed my eyes at my aunt. "You're literally killing me."

"That's not what *literally* means. This social media thing is really destroying your generation's language-arts know-how."

"Ugh!" I repeated, this time loud enough that Ollie pulled off his headphones again.

"Is the pizza here now?"

Maddie and I both laughed this time. Pepper gave a short bark at the indignity of having her bed jostled twice in five minutes.

"Well, that's one benefit of being sessile. He makes a great dog bed," Maddie observed.

"What's *sessile* mean?"

"See? Social media generation. Why don't you look it up while I make the pizza delivery time earlier so Ollie doesn't die of hunger?"

I grabbed my phone. "Siri, what does sessile mean?" I asked.

SESSILE MEANS PERMANENTLY ATTACHED, NOT FREELY MOVING, LIKE A BARNACLE OR OTHER SEA CREATURE ON A FIXED STALK.

I glanced at Maddie. "You know that's not *literally* true of Oliver," I said.

Maddie looked over at my brother. He'd lain back down on the floor, and Pepper had moved onto his belly.

Maddie shrugged. "Not *yet*."

While Maddie was busy with the food delivery app on her phone, I went back to looking (casually) at Jai's Relay page. I noticed an old picture of Jai posing with an unknown girl in what looked like a school cafeteria decorated with streamers. He was wearing a suit, and the girl was wearing a beautiful pink party dress. She was very pretty, with long, dark brown hair and brown skin. Jai had tagged her; her Relay screen name was @AmaraS06. Jai had captioned the picture: Flashback to junior #HOCO hijinks!!

Junior homecoming? Was this Jai's girlfriend?

My first thought was to text Nina and ask her opinion, but then I decided that I was being ridiculous. What did it even matter if Amara S. were Jai's girlfriend? He and I weren't . . . we were just sort of becoming friends.

"That's a nice dress," Maddie said, giving me a heart attack. She was looking at the picture of Amara. "Sorry, I didn't mean to spy," my aunt added.

I nodded. "It's okay. It *would* be fun to wear a dress like that to an event sometime," I admitted to my aunt. I explained to her how plain I'd felt in my cater-waiter costume at Sarah's bat mitzvah while Nina and the other girls had been in cute dresses. Maddie nodded sympathetically.

Just then, a text came in from Nina; she must have just woken up in California. She'd been faithful about texting me pictures of her meals: So far there'd been a poke bowl, fish tacos, and some tasty-looking shawarma. Today there was no picture yet.

Update on pugs + cute singer asap plz & thank u.

No one came forward for pugs but keep your fingers crossed. Aunt Maddie is here so she might help me work on Mom. Jai is still cute, also still a singer.

Smarty-pants. Update on YOU TWO. Also keeping fingers + toes crossed u get to keep pugs!!!!!!!!!!!!!!

He sent me a direct Relay! But mostly just talking about his dog & pugs.

You send him one! We are about to go to the beach but will text later.

I texted Nina back a smiley face, then put my phone and laptop away. I needed to take Pepper and Jack outside, and I didn't want Maddie bugging me any more about being too attached to my social media.

10

Admit It

I woke up the next morning feeling tired. I'd had trouble falling asleep, even when I'd tried to read one of the summer reading books we'd been assigned, which was about women wearing petticoats and having tea while searching for husbands.

I had a lot on my mind, I realized as I went downstairs to get the pugs out of their crate. Besides the usual worries about the pugs, I was upset that Maddie would be going back to Orlando today. And I was also wondering who exactly that mystery girl was on Jai's Relay page.

After the dogs had their breakfast and walk, I decided to do what always helped ease my worries: cook. We had another big event coming up—another wedding; it was the season—and it wasn't too soon to start experimenting. Mom had agreed that I could design two completely different dishes. My ideas were to make grilled chicken skewers with a sauce made from sambal oelek, which is a chili sauce similar to sriracha (but better). And then, miniature steak-and-oyster pies. The pizzazz for that one was something I was particularly proud of: a dash of chili powder.

I went into the kitchen to start making the pies. Making the pastry from scratch was the part I was a little worried about, but it was kind of exciting, too, trying something new. Pepper and Jack were just as excited, judging by the way they kept dancing around my legs, their tails two wagging blurs. I was pretty sure they were just hoping I'd drop some food, but I'd take all the support I could get.

I got flour on myself, and all over the puppies' heads, backs, and tails. I snapped a pic of a flour-covered Jack to post on Relay later—he'd managed to get much messier than his sister. Then when I was done making the pastry, I had to wipe each pug off with a wet paper towel.

Mom came into the kitchen and grinned when she saw I'd already made her coffee.

Okay, so maybe I was making a little bit of a special effort to be a good kid, and take care of more than just Pepper and Jack. I'd been holding my breath waiting for Mom to mention keeping—or not keeping—the pugs. But when she didn't bring it up, I was afraid to. Maybe she'd be so busy working she'd keep forgetting for the rest of the summer. And by then we'd just *have* to keep the pups, was my thinking.

That afternoon, we had a special goodbye lunch for Maddie, and I served my steak-and-oyster pies. But I made a special pie with mushrooms for Ollie, since I knew he didn't like oysters.

"Aw, thanks for making it special for your brother, Sam," Dad told me. "You know, you tried your first raw oyster when you were only three years old. And you loved it, too!"

Ollie looked kind of hurt that Dad was bragging about my adventurous eating. Ollie, on the other hand, had always been a picky eater—the only one in the family. I was reminded of the conversation Aunt Maddie and I had had about Ollie yesterday.

I dug in to eat. I was relieved that the pie had a good flavor, and Dad had made a nice spinach salad to go on the side. Maddie, Mom, and Dad all complimented the dish and I felt a happy glow.

"Sam, there's something I wanted to mention to you," Mom said as we were washing dishes. "And also, why are you washing the dishes? You cooked!"

I shrugged. "Well, I made the dishes dirty. You know how many forks I use." It was a family joke that I would routinely use every single fork, and most of the spoons, in the flatware drawer while cooking. I always forget I already have one out and just grab a new one.

"Okay, fair point. But I was going to tell you that you don't need to serve at our next event. It's a buffet, and we have plenty of staff helping." Mom paused, then added, "You should be spending time with kids your own age."

I saw Mom exchange a look with Aunt Maddie. I could smell that something was up.

I turned to my aunt. "Just what, exactly, have you been telling her?"

Maddie made an innocent face and asked, "What do you mean?"

"You know what I mean."

Jack gave a short, urgent-sounding bark just then, and I knew what *that* meant, so I grabbed both the dogs' leashes. "Saved by the bark," Maddie said under her breath.

After I came back inside with the dogs—Pepper took a ridiculous amount of time choosing a location—we all said goodbye to Maddie, who was packed up and ready to get in her car. I gave her an extra-long hug, even though I was still suspicious about what she might have said to Mom about me. But still, as always, I was grateful to my aunt for everything.

The next day, I sat on the sofa with Pepper and Jack on either side of me as I scrolled through Relay. Nobody had come forward as the pugs' owner yet, but they were getting tons of likes and comments on all their pictures. I'd reposted all the cute photos of them onto their profile, and also added a new one from last night: I'd put both pugs in the upstairs tub, along with a bunch of bath toys I found under the sink that were leftover from when Ollie was little. The latest adorableness was getting more likes than ever.

"But where did you two come from?" I asked Pepper and Jack, as if they could really answer me. Pepper only barked, and Jack lazily wagged his tail.

I was about to text Nina to see what she was up to in California when the doorbell rang. I wondered if it was a food delivery for Mom and Dad. Or maybe, I thought nervously as I ran to the door, it was someone finally coming to claim the pugs.

Instead, it was the FedEx man, dropping off a package. I was stunned to see that the package was addressed to me. I carefully used scissors to cut it open, and Pepper and Jack played with the box—perhaps remembering their old box—while I pulled out the item inside.

It was a dress. A really pretty, dark blue dress, just my size. And there was a card in the box that read: *Dear Sam, Consider this a very early birthday present. XO Aunt Maddie*

Maddie! I couldn't believe it. I remembered how she'd seen me looking at the Relay picture of Amara S., and how I'd confided in her that I wished I'd had a nice dress. She must have ordered this dress online before she went back to Orlando yesterday.

My aunt had figured out what I hadn't even totally admitted to myself: that I really wanted to wear something nice to the next event. So that Jai could see me in something other than a boring old cater-waiter outfit . . .

Uh-oh.

I grabbed my phone. I needed to call Maddie to thank her, but first I *had* to text Nina. I sent her a picture of the dress, and the words that had just echoed in my brain: Uh-oh.

Nina wrote back right away.

What? It's really pretty—where did u get it?

I didn't get it—it was Maddie!! But that's not the UH-OH . . .

Well????????

I think I might like Jai.

Yeah. Duh.

WHATTTTT????????????? You knew?!?!

Sure did. Why uh-oh? He's super cute and nice—&
seems 2 like u!

I've never really liked anybody like that before. Now I feel
like I'm gonna be weird around him ☹

Relax friend. You=awesome and he is lucky YOU like
HIM :} Now I'm gonna go eat sushi <3 xoxo

I sat down on the floor and leaned back against the couch.
While I appreciated my best friend's pep talk, I still felt a ton of
nervous energy coursing through me. I couldn't believe I'd just
confessed to liking Jai—even just on text to Nina.

I called Aunt Maddie and it went to voice mail, so I left her
a message telling her how much I loved the dress. Then I brought
Pepper and Jack upstairs with me so I could try the dress on in
my room.

It fit well, and it was a great dress—simple but with a nice
flare to the skirt part. My very own non-uniform outfit to wear
to the next event. I looked in the mirror and decided I looked
good. So why did I feel even more nervous about the idea of seeing Jai while wearing *this* than I would in my usual outfit?

I pulled the dress over my head and took it off, hanging it back up and trying to ignore the strange clothing paradox I'd just discovered.

I had trouble falling asleep again. So that night, for the first time, I cheated on Mom's new plan to keep Pepper and Jack in their crate overnight. I crept downstairs, opened the crate, scooped up one pug in each arm, and went back upstairs.

"Love you guys. Don't forget, okay?" I told them as we snuggled in for the night.

11

Runaway Slug

"Wow, Sam, you clean up nice!" Jai said when he saw me walk into the hotel in my new dress.

Even though being told I was clean wasn't exactly the compliment of my dreams, I still felt my cheeks turn warm. I heard a snort behind me, and looked back to see Ollie. As usual, he was glued to his gaming device. But he was still paying enough attention to his surroundings to embarrass me. Why, oh why, did I get a great dress to wear on the one hand, but then get stuck with Captain Annoying on the other hand?

This event—another wedding—was being held at a huge hotel and golf resort on the north end of Palm Beach. Before we'd left home, I'd packed up Pepper and Jack along with their food, crate, beds, water bowl, treats, and toys (I'd finally convinced Dad to let me buy them some real dog toys). Mom had packed up Ollie with basically the same sort of thing: his gaming system and charger, snacks, and a pillow. I'd stashed the dogs in a far corner of the kitchen while Mom and Dad set up, and now Ollie was following me around.

"Thanks," I told Jai as I crossed the ballroom toward him. He was wearing a tux, like he had at the last wedding.

"No catering uniform tonight?" Jai asked me.

I blushed again, and shrugged. "My mom said I don't need to serve at this event. So I figured, why not?" It wasn't *completely* a lie.

I heard another snort from behind me.

"Oliver, right?" Jai said, and Ollie's head snapped up. I prayed he wouldn't say anything to embarrass me further. "You helping out the fam tonight?" Jai asked him.

"Nah," Ollie replied. "I mean, I don't, like, cook or anything."

"I can't cook, either," Jai said. "Not even toast. Burn it every time."

Ollie smiled at Jai. That was new. My little brother usually wore a look of grim concentration that I would describe as his video-game face, but a real smile from him was pretty rare. Trust Jai, who charmed everybody, to coax one out of him.

"You know, the Calloway bunch may not need any help, but the Jams clan could use some," Jai said to Ollie. "What do you say, any interest in learning how to be a roadie for the band? I could show you a few basics. You'd really be helping us out."

There was that smile again, and Ollie surprised me by saying "Sure!" to Jai.

Jai smiled at me and then left with Ollie to finish setting up their equipment. I went to check on Pepper and Jack, who were happily playing with their new toys in the crate. Mom and Dad were sending the appetizers out with the servers, so I went back to the ballroom to check out the reception and the music.

Dr. Jams was onstage with the whole band, including Jai, and they were playing a fun song that had everyone in the crowd dancing. I noticed Ollie up there, too, clapping his hands to the beat in a corner of the stage. He looked happier than he had in a while. Then Dr. Jams gave the microphone to Jai, and he announced that he was going to teach the crowd to do a Bollywood dance. People clapped excitedly.

And then I heard it:

"Sam Calloway!" Jai called into the microphone. "I'm going to need you to come on up here. Ladies and gentlemen, one of the chefs tonight—let's give her a round of applause and convince her to come on up here and dance with us!"

I froze. No way! I couldn't do that.

But everyone in the audience was cheering for me. And I saw Ollie waving to me from the stage.

Somehow, to my surprise, I found myself with a heated face making my way toward the stage. I walked up nervously, but Jai greeted me with a big smile, and Ollie stepped up beside me.

"I'm gonna try it, too, Sam!" Ollie told me with a grin.

Dr. J and the band started playing the music as Jai demonstrated the steps and arm movements for the audience.

I followed along. I felt awkward trying the moves, but with my usually slug-like little brother trying it beside me, I knew I really had no excuse. Dr. J came over at one point and fixed my hand movements, which was embarrassing, but before long, I was laughing and dancing along with the rest of the crowd. I couldn't believe it. Me, shy Sam Calloway, was up onstage dancing—and it was so fun I forgot to feel mortified. I'd have to tell Nina.

After the Bollywood number was over, everyone clapped and then went to eat dinner. The band took a break then, so Jai joined me in the kitchen to visit the pugs. Ollie trailed behind us, but then went to go sit in a corner of the kitchen with his pillow and video games.

"That was a really cool dance," I told Jai as I opened the crate and let the pugs come out. "I've seen Bollywood dancing in movies and stuff but I never thought I'd be doing one. Or trying to."

"You were great for a first-timer," Jai said, scratching Jack behind the ears. "Back home we have a small community of Indians, but we're all very close. Everyone is invited to everyone else's weddings, engagement parties, birthdays, anniversaries. And everyone is always dancing."

My mind flashed back to the girl from his Relay page. She had appeared to be Indian, too. And then I was picturing them dancing together. Maybe at his school's homecoming dance.

I shook my head to try to clear away the image. "Have you ever been to India?" I asked Jai. I didn't have the guts to ask what I really kind of wanted to: *What's up with you and the super-pretty Amara S.?*

Jai shook his head sadly. "No. I was born here—I mean, back home in Maryland. But I really want to go to India. After I graduate from high school I'm planning to take a year and go. I've already started saving."

"That's so cool," I said. Pepper licked my hand, and I giggled. "After high school, I want to go to culinary school. Not that that's highly surprising."

"No, not a huge shock," he agreed with a smile. "Me, on the other hand; I'm not sure what I want to study. I want to go to a performing arts high school, so I can keep singing and acting. But there are a lot of fields I'm interested in. Screenwriting, and film studies. And I love studying history." Jai looked over at me while he fed Jack a treat. "I know cooking is, like, your main thing, but is there anything else you'd want to do?"

I thought about his question. For as long as I could remember, cooking had been my passion, overshadowing everything else. But what if I couldn't cook anymore? What would I be interested in? All of a sudden, compared to Jai's list of interests, I felt like a boring one-channel TV. Which actually reminded me of a dream I'd had when I was younger.

"I used to want to have my own cooking show," I confessed. "I mean, I know that's sort of the same thing, but I was actually really into the idea when I was younger. I thought I could have a show where I told funny stories about the food I made. I don't know, it's silly . . ." I looked down at the pugs.

"That's not silly. I think you'd be great at that. You're really funny."

I definitely turned red then. "No one's ever told me that. I mean, thank you."

"You're welcome. It's totally true. What would you call the show?"

"I don't know. *Not* Shrimp Sam."

He laughed. "You'll think of something."

I glanced over at Ollie in the corner, still absorbed in his video game. "Hey," I told Jai. "Thanks for pretending to let my brother help earlier."

Jai frowned. "I wasn't pretending."

I was going to ask him what he meant, but then I heard Dr. Jams calling to him from the ballroom, so I knew his break was over.

"See you later!" Jai called, running back out the door. "I'll come back to visit the pugs!"

I nodded, feeling uncertain about what I'd said about Ollie. Jai was an only child, though, so he probably just didn't understand how annoying little brothers could be.

My parents came into the kitchen then, looking harried.

"Sam, I'm glad you're here," Mom said. "Please put the pugs away and wash your hands. The bride and groom want some more of those stuffed mushroom appetizers. Would you mind whipping up a few more for us now? We have to finish up the dinner service."

"Sure," I said. Dad handed me a spare apron, and I got to work. My parents headed back into the ballroom to check on the dinner service.

"Hey, Ollie, can you come over here and help me a little?" I asked my brother. Of course, I got no answer since he was wearing headphones, so I had to wipe off my hands, walk over there, and tap him on the shoulder. "Ollie! Come help me."

"What do you need my help for? You're the perfect gourmet chef."

"Well, I'm a gourmet chef who's running out of time. Here, I need you to pull all these mushroom stems off, but you have to pull carefully, like this." I demonstrated, then put the cap down on the lined baking sheet I'd already prepared. Ollie groaned and picked up a mushroom, moving at whatever was the opposite of lightning speed. "Can you pick up the pace a little? Why do you always have to be such a slug?" I groaned.

Ollie picked up another mushroom and ripped off the stem—fast this time, but he split the entire cap apart while he was doing it. "Not like that—you ruined the cap! Never mind, I'll do it myself. As always." I shouldered him out of the way, and he went. I figured he'd gone back to his corner, or maybe out to the ballroom to visit Jai.

It wasn't until I'd finished the stuffed mushrooms and sent them out with a server that Mom came to find me, frantically grabbing my arm and asking, "Where's Ollie?"

"What do you mean? He's right there." I turned and pointed, but he wasn't in his corner. "Oh. Is he out on the stage with Jai?"

Mom shook her head. "We checked there, too. Your father hasn't seen him, either. It's been at least an hour. Where can he be?"

"Mom, calm down," I said, wiping my hands on a dish towel. "He has to be around here somewhere. He doesn't have a car or anything."

"Sam, this property is huge! He could have wandered off anywhere . . ."

"Mom, this is a swanky golf resort. I don't think you need to worry he's been kidnapped by maniacs or anything."

"This isn't a time for you to joke!" Mom's voice went up at least an octave, and several of the servers in the kitchen turned to stare at us.

"I wasn't trying to make a joke," I said quietly, feeling bad. "I'll see if I can go find him, okay?"

I hurried out of the kitchen, annoyed. Ollie was truly unbelievable. When I had the nerve to ask him to help out with one tiny thing, he couldn't even do it right. And now he'd wandered off, and I had to find him.

I realized I didn't hear the band playing, so I headed back behind the stage area to look for Jai. Maybe Ollie *had* gone to help Jai again.

"Hey, Jai—are you on a break?" I asked when I found him. He nodded, and I asked, "Have you seen Ollie?"

Jai shook his head. "Your parents were asking my dad about him, too. What's going on?"

I shrugged. "Seems like my brother decided to pull a disappearing act."

"Wait, what? Your brother is missing?" Jai sounded genuinely concerned.

"I mean, he's not actually *missing*—he's just wandered off somewhere, and I told my mom I'd track him down."

"Certainly sounds like *missing*," Jai observed. "I'll help you find him. We can take a golf cart—Dad and I borrowed one earlier to move speakers and we've still got the keys. We can cover more ground faster."

"Okay, great." Getting to ride around with Jai in a golf cart didn't sound so bad. Maybe Ollie should go missing more often.

I waited outside the building while Jai went to get the golf cart. When he drove up, I climbed into the seat beside him.

"Where did you see him last?" Jai's hands were poised on the wheel.

"In the kitchen. But I don't know which way he headed."

"Well, then, I guess we pick a direction and just start there. North or south?"

"North," I said. I had no idea which was even which from this vantage point, but Jai seemed to know. He pulled away and we went driving into the evening.

We drove along in silence for a few moments. I racked my brain trying to come up with something to say. I settled for: "Thanks for helping me find Ollie. He's so unbelievably annoying."

"What did he do?" Jai asked, sounding surprised.

"He didn't *do* anything, that's the problem. He basically just takes up space. I asked him to help with one tiny, easy thing, and he couldn't even be bothered."

"Was it a cooking thing?"

"No, I asked him to do some juggling. Of course it was a *cooking thing*. It is the family business."

I bit my lip. I hadn't meant to be *quite* so sarcastic. I was clearly on edge.

"Sam, I know you love all things cooking," Jai said slowly as we bumped along the road. "But Ollie clearly doesn't. And since that's the main thing your family does, he probably feels pretty left out."

"He told you that?"

"He didn't have to. I can see it."

I crossed my arms over my chest, feeling defensive. "Jai, no offense or anything, but you barely know my brother. How would you have some great insight that I don't have—or my parents?"

"Have I told you why I'm here this summer, in Florida?"

I narrowed my eyes in confusion at the sudden change in

topic. Jai didn't look at me as he was turning the golf cart around to search in a different part of the resort.

"You're here to visit your dad," I said.

"Yeah, but I didn't tell you why. See, the thing is, my mother got remarried this spring. To a guy who's younger than her—she and all her friends think he's really handsome. She was really excited about her new life. And the guy—he's nice enough, I guess, but apparently he felt like it would be good if I were gone for a while, just at the beginning. So, my mom sent me to Florida to live with my dad for the summer."

Oh. I blinked. I hadn't known any of that. "I'm sorry, Jai," I said softly. "That sounds hard to go through."

He nodded, looking ahead. "Thanks. Yeah."

"But," I said, trying to look on the bright side, "your dad's great . . ."

"He's a great guy, a great performer, but he hasn't always been the best father, Sam. My mom tried other summers to get him to invite me here, but he almost never took the bait. This year, she didn't give him a choice. She basically just said, 'Jai's coming, here's when his flight lands, pick him up at the airport.'"

Jai let out a breath. He'd been talking quickly, like he wanted to spill out everything before he lost his nerve.

I didn't know how to respond. "Why are you telling me all of this right now?" I finally asked, feeling awkward.

"Because I feel like I sort of understand what Ollie's going through. Not feeling wanted."

"No one ever said they didn't *want* him!" I protested.

Jai stopped the golf cart and looked at me. "Okay, so you didn't say you didn't want him. What did you say to him, though, Sam?"

I shrugged, feeling a tiny bit sheepish. "I asked him to do a decent job and stop being a slug . . ."

"You called your little brother a slug?"

"He IS a slug, Jai—you have no idea what you're talking about here . . ."

Jai swallowed. "Let me get this straight. I tell you every painful detail about how my mom didn't want me at home, and this is how you respond? I'm beginning to see why Ollie felt the need to take off."

My face felt red and hot. I couldn't just sit there beside him any longer, not with his words still hanging in the air between us.

I jumped out of the golf cart. "Fine. Whatever, Jai. Let's just pretend that since you have your own family drama that you totally understand mine. I'll just go find my brother myself. I'm sorry I bothered you."

Jai looked at me once more. He shook his head, but didn't say anything else before he drove the golf cart away. I realized after he'd gone that it had gotten dark and I had no flashlight. Which seemed like a completely perfect end to a completely terrible day.

12

Maybe Jai Was Wrong

"And, because the universe hates me, it was Jai who found Ollie anyway, so then the little monster got to have a fun golf cart ride back to the hotel. Jai even let him *drive*!"

On my laptop screen, Nina raised her eyebrows at me. "So where was Ollie the whole time?"

I took a breath and sat back on my bed. Nina was still in California, and I'd asked if we could Skype so I could fill her in on what had happened with Ollie and Jai last night.

"He was sitting under a tree on the golf course, feeling sorry for himself because the battery on his game had run out." I sighed. "That's not the point!"

"It's not?" Nina frowned. "Weren't you worried about him?"

"Of course I was!" I cried. "Great, you probably think I'm a horrible person now, too. Jai certainly does. Not that it matters. I just won't talk to him and before we know it he'll be going back home anyway. And I say good riddance."

Nina rolled her eyes. "I don't think you're a horrible person, Sam. Can you stop being so dramatic? But wow, Jai really got under your skin."

"He did not!" I protested. Pepper, who'd been napping at the foot of my bed, gave a start and woke up, and I realized I'd yelled pretty loud. "I'm just—annoyed," I said, trying to sound calmer. "Jai went so crazy defending my little brother, acting like I'm some terrible sister or something." I exhaled and looked at Nina and said in a smaller voice, "I don't think I'm a terrible sister."

"You're not a terrible sister. But you and Ollie don't really have, like, a close relationship. Maybe it would make you feel better if you spent some more time with him."

"I knew it! You agree with Jai."

Nina shook her head. "I don't agree with him. You're right, Jai's not in your family, and it was pretty unfair for him to say that he understands how Ollie feels because he's having some issues with his own mom." Nina gave me a knowing look. "But, Sam, if you're getting this upset, I have to wonder if it's not because part of you feels like there's a grain of truth to what Jai was telling you."

I hugged my knees to my chest. "I don't know. You have two older siblings who are super cool. You don't really understand, either, Nina."

"I didn't say that I did," she responded, sounding a little hurt.

"I'm sorry," I said right away. "I didn't mean that last part. Promise." I frowned. "I'm just . . . I thought I liked Jai. And I kind of thought that maybe, possibly . . . he kind of liked me, too."

"I know, Sam. I'm sorry."

"It's not your fault. Thanks for letting me vent. And I'm sorry for being a butt."

"You're not a butt. You just need something to get your mind off all this. Luckily, I'm back next week. And then, remember? Comedy retreat, baby!"

Oh, right. Last month, Nina had signed us both up for a summer improv retreat, and I'd reluctantly agreed and gotten the sign-off from my parents. Nina was certain that she could get me to love doing improvisational comedy as much as she did, and then join the In-Betweeners with her when school started again.

"I don't know if I can go through with that," I said.

"Of course you can!" Nina told me. "Besides, weren't you just saying you felt boring because you only focus on cooking?"

I shrugged. I had told Nina about that part of last night, too, when I'd compared myself to Jai and all his interests.

"This will be a chance for you to try something new," Nina said.

"Maybe," I said. I smiled and raised my water bottle to cheers with her. Maybe my best friend was right. Maybe a distraction, like embarrassing myself in front of the school's comedy troupe, was just what I needed.

"Sam!" my mom called from downstairs. I told Nina I had to

go, and I logged off. I kissed the pugs on their heads and returned them to their crate, and then I ran downstairs.

I found Mom, Dad, and Ollie all sitting around the kitchen table. They looked like they'd been waiting for me.

"Have a seat, Sam," Mom said. "We need to have a family meeting."

She said this like "family meetings" were a thing that we regularly had, but we'd never had one before in my whole life.

"What's up?" I asked, taking my seat beside Ollie. His head was down and he was playing with a loose thread on the seat cushion.

"Sam, *what's up* is that your little brother ran away last night and we need to have a discussion about that. All of us," Mom said sharply.

"Why all of us? I didn't do anything. Last night I was exactly where I was supposed to be—just like I always am!"

Mom opened her mouth as if to continue, but Dad put a hand on her arm and spoke next. "We know that you were, Sam, but Oliver taking off like that, it's a big deal. Something bad could have happened. We're lucky that it didn't, but we still need to stop and take stock. The fact is that we've been spending so much time at events, or getting ready for events, that we've let family go by the wayside. And that's on your mother and me. But we all need to be a part of repairing things. This is something we need to do as a family. All of us." He repeated Mom's words.

"Okay, I get that," I said in a calmer voice. The weird tension when I'd walked in, followed by Mom's words, had taken me right back to my fight with Jai the night before. But maybe Jai had been wrong. Dad had said that what happened with Ollie was on him and Mom—not me. What did Jai know anyway? He wasn't in this family. Surely my *parents* knew best. They were the grown-ups, after all.

I tuned back in to what Dad was saying. He seemed to have taken over running the "family meeting." Knowing the two of them, they'd probably arranged to have him—the calmer one—do the talking all along, but then Mom hadn't been able to help herself. I knew which one of them I took after in this case, I thought to myself. I would have jumped in, too.

". . . so your mother and I have decided that a family vacation would be a good first step," Dad was saying. "It will have to be a short one, maybe just for the weekend—so we'll have to drive. It's too late to buy plane tickets this time. Do either of you have any ideas of places that you would like to go?"

Ollie kept plucking at the loose thread. Dad looked at me.

"Maybe Ollie should pick," I said.

Now we were all staring at the top of Ollie's blond head, which I knew he was hating. Maybe suggesting that he pick wasn't the nice thing to do after all.

"Ollie, we had fun in St. Augustine that time, remember?" I prompted.

It was actually the only family trip I could really remember. But we *had* had fun, playing road trip games in the car, eating seafood, and playing on the beach. Sure, we also had had a beach twenty minutes from home, but we never went there as a family—unless it was to cater an event at a beachfront property, that is.

Ollie nodded and finally looked up. "Yeah, that was fun."

And so, it was decided. We were going on a (long, as I remembered) car trip up to St. Augustine. "The dogs can come, right?" I asked.

"Or we could see about boarding them," Dad said.

"They're too little." We all looked in surprise at Ollie, who'd spoken up. "We should bring them."

I grinned at my brother.

"Okay, then it's settled," Mom said. "It'd be expensive to board them anyway. Sam, that reminds me, I made a vet appointment for the dogs for tomorrow morning at nine. It's past time we get them checked out and get them their shots and . . . whatever else they need."

"Wow, thanks, Mom. I'll have them all ready in their travel crate."

"I'm sure you will. Okay, gang. Good first family meeting. I guess it's adjourned, though."

We all stayed in our chairs. "What did I forget?" Mom asked.

Dad laughed. "Ironically enough, you forgot about dinner. But no worries—I'll order us a pizza."

Mom chuckled. "Sorry. One-track mind."

Dad kissed the top of her head and chuckled. "And for once it wasn't on food."

His words kept echoing in my head as I fed and walked Pepper and Jack. Maybe I was even more like Mom than I'd realized—a one-track mind, usually stuck on food.

But at least one thing had been helped by the family meeting: I felt better about where things stood with Ollie. If only I could feel better about Jai, too.

13
Slightly French

Ollie surprised me—and Mom—by wanting to go with us to the vet's office the next morning. So the three of us piled into the car, with me holding Jack and Ollie holding Pepper. Mom insisted that we put their travel carrier in the trunk, just in case. I held Jack up so he could look out the window, and I vowed to come back out to the car after we got home to Windex off the slobber stains he was leaving. Dad was laid-back about everything except the car.

Mom had called her friend who has three dogs to get a vet recommendation, and it turned out the vet had been their mutual friend from high school. So when we got to the vet's office, Dr. Martinez came out from the back right away and hugged Mom and they spent a long time gabbing before she took us back to an exam room.

"Oh, what beautiful pugs! But I have to say, Missy, I'm kind of surprised at you having *two* dogs!" Dr. Martinez exclaimed. "Your mom was always a neat freak, and everything had to be in order," she told Ollie and me. "Dogs bring chaos, as I'm sure you're finding out."

"They were a bit of an accident—someone left them on our porch," Mom told her. "And the kids fell in love. But they have been a big help with them."

Mom certainly was talking like the pugs were staying. I felt a rush of hope.

Dr. Martinez checked out each dog, shining a light into their eyes and ears and feeling down their spines. "They seem very healthy; they're at a good weight. Since you found them, we should check for microchips. We have a scanner."

I felt a cold tug of fear. *Oh no*—I hadn't considered that Pepper and Jack could have those chips that owners use to track their pets. What if they had them? I looked at Mom in panic, but she was already saying, "Yes, of course we need to check."

"If they don't have chips, we should probably assume they're not up-to-date on their shots. Hold on, I'll be right back." Dr. Martinez opened the door and called out for someone, then a younger woman wearing scrubs printed with paws and dog bones came back in with her. "This is Beth, one of our vet techs. She's going to help me get these guys weighed and scanned in the back." She turned to Beth. "Aren't these such cute pugs? They just found them on their porch—can you believe someone abandoning purebred dogs like that?"

Beth was holding Jack up with his face close to hers. "They are adorable, but they're not purebred." She turned to Mom. "I hope you're not disappointed, but these two definitely have at least a little bit of French bulldog in them."

Dr. Martinez nodded. "Beth knows what she's talking about—she and her husband breed pugs and dachshunds."

"It's a fairly popular combo," Beth went on. "Pugs and French bulldogs, I mean. They call them Frenchie-Pugs or Frugs."

"Frugs?" I repeated, and Ollie started laughing. I elbowed him.

"Yep." Beth smiled. "My guess is that one parent was a Frug—which makes them at least three-quarter pug. They'll look like pugs to anyone who's not an expert. But you can't show them."

"Show them?" Ollie asked. "What do you mean?"

"Like in a dog show," I explained.

Mom laughed. "We were never going to do that."

"Okay, well, we'll be right back," Beth said, and she and Dr. Martinez carried Pepper and Jack away. I waved to them so they wouldn't be scared.

"I can't believe they might be microchipped," I said when the two left the exam room. I didn't care much about the Frug thing—I was still fixated on the chip thing. I started pacing in the small space, then practically ran into Ollie because it turned out he was doing the same thing. We exchanged a look, and he looked worried, too. I guessed he'd gotten more attached to the pups than I'd realized.

The wait seemed to take forever, but finally Beth and Dr. Martinez came back.

"Okay, we're good to go," Dr. Martinez said. "No chips, and we gave them their first round of shots: distemper, measles, and parainfluenza."

I sagged against the cold metal exam table in relief and Mom gave me a smile. Even Ollie was smiling. And Pepper and Jack were thrilled to be done with their tests and shots; they bounded into my arms and greeted me with licks and thumping tails. We finished up at the vet and headed home.

When we got back, Mom dropped us off along with Pepper and Jack, and headed back out to Whole Foods. Ollie carried Pepper again while I carried Jack.

Ollie surprised me yet again when we walked inside and he announced, "I know what you've been doing, sneaking the dogs upstairs after Mom and Dad go to bed."

"What? How?" I thought I'd been so stealthy. I'd gotten away with it so far because I've pretty much always had trouble falling asleep—it's just hard for me to get my mind to stop going over and over everything that happened that day, and everything that was coming up the next day. So, it was easy as anything to stay awake later than our parents and come back down to get the dogs out of their crate. I actually slept a lot better once I had their warm, comforting little bodies to snuggle up to. Jack had even taken to sleeping with his little head on the edge of my pillow.

Of course, on the flip side, having dogs in bed with you meant no sleeping late, even in summer, because they will wake you up with face licks if necessary. By the time it's light out, they're ready to eat breakfast and go outside. This fact allowed me to beat Mom and Dad back down in the morning, since catering is usually a late-night business.

"Are you saying this because you're planning to tell on me?" I asked my brother. I wondered if he wanted something in exchange for his silence.

"No, I just want in. I want Pepper to stay with me."

I stared at him. I had noticed that he'd been bonding a lot with Pepper lately, but still, I was surprised. "Ollie, I can sneak down to get them because I have so much trouble going to sleep— you know that. You fall asleep watching TV. It's easy for you."

"I figured that's how you were doing it, and you can bring her in to me and wake me up. I don't mind."

"Okay, but have you also noticed how early they get me up in the mornings? When school starts back up it won't be that big a deal, but if you do keep Pepper with you at night, she's going to wake you up early in the morning to be fed and walked. She might even wake you up sooner than Jack wakes me—she's usually the first one up. Then you'd have to handle everything . . ."

"I get it. I mean, I don't care. I'll get up. Promise."

I looked at him for a few seconds. "Okay. I mean, they're your dogs, too."

"They are? I mean, I kind of thought you felt like they were just yours . . ."

I thought about that for a moment. "Yeah, that's fair. I kind of did. But if you want to help more, and you want to keep Pepper at night, I'm totally fine with that." Maybe helping to take care of them could teach my little brother some responsibility. "They *should* be both our dogs," I told him.

Ollie gave me another one of those rare smiles. "Great!" He hugged Pepper close and started talking to her. "You hear that, Pep? You're going to hang with me at night from now on!"

"I should take them out," I said.

And then Ollie surprised me a *third* time by saying, "I'll do it."

Wow, this whole learning-responsibility thing sure was kicking in fast!

14

Road Trip, with Puppies

"Everything's on my side!" I shoved the cooler at my feet over toward Ollie's side of the back seat. "You have more room."

"Do not! I've got a ton of crap under my feet!" he shouted back at me.

"Children!" our father yelled from the driver's seat. "Don't make me pull this car over." He turned to glance at Mom. "Great, now I've turned into my father."

"I think car trips bring that out in a family," Mom told him.

"We should have brought the van," I grumbled, wriggling in my seat so that the big duffel bag between me and Ollie wouldn't poke me in the side. Pepper and Jack, in their crate, barked and whined as the car went over a bump in the road.

"I guess maybe we should have," Mom agreed. "But it's too late now. Let's just try to make the best of it, okay?"

I groaned. "Trade seats with me and then we'll talk."

"Sam," Dad said. "Be nice to your mom."

"Sorry," I said.

"Why don't you get the pups out of their crate?" Mom suggested.

"I thought you said they needed to stay in there, for safety or something . . ."

"I changed my mind," Mom interrupted, her voice sounding brittle.

So I opened up the little wire door to the travel crate. I handed Ollie his favorite, Pepper, and I picked up Jack and accepted the massive face licking he gave me for letting him out.

The miles started to pass much more pleasantly, and I took tons of cute pictures of the traveling pups on my phone. I uploaded the cutest one, of Ollie cuddling with Pepper, with the caption: Hugs from pugs make the miles go faster.

It was almost five o'clock when we reached St. Augustine. Dad had a little trouble finding the condo we had rented—pet-friendly, of course—with a kitchen (which explained all the extra stuff Mom had felt the need to pack). Once we parked, we unloaded everything and carried our bags and dogs inside.

Ollie and I had to share a room with bunk beds (yay) and we would have the pugs sleep on a blanket on the floor right by us. Mom made us a simple dinner of yummy quesadillas while we unpacked, and then we went out for a walk with the puppies. The condo was close enough to the beach that we could easily walk there. It was funny, I thought; this was the same beach we had at home, but it seemed more exotic way up north. And the pugs loved the beach; they dove in and out of the sand, and Pepper was even brave enough to dip her paws in the water (Jack didn't dare).

When we got back from our walk, we made s'mores around the condo's firepit, and soon Jack was positively obsessed with marshmallows. They kept getting stuck in his teeth and it was hysterical watching him chew and chew. I took a picture of him begging for more (#marshmallowhound) and posted it.

Mom and Dad went to bed, and Ollie and I stayed up late telling ghost stories in our bunk beds. Then we settled Pepper and Jack down on their blanket. The final pic of the night showed the two adorable siblings cuddled up to go to sleep.

"Hey, Sam?"

I was starting to drift off to sleep. "Yeah, Ollie?" I asked.

"Thanks for letting me share the pugs," he said.

"Welcome," I told him. And I meant it. That was the nice thing about puppy love, I reflected. Sharing it just seemed to make more love to go around. "Good night, Pepper and Jack," I called.

Thank goodness Ollie left the porch unlocked that day, was my last thought as I drifted off to sleep.

15

Beach Break and Best Friends

When I came back from St. Augustine, Nina was already back from California, so we immediately made plans to meet up. Ollie said he'd watch Pepper and Jack, so Nina's mom picked me up and drove Nina and me to the beach. Nina and I caught up in the car, filling each other in on our respective trips. But we didn't *really* start catching up until Mrs. Katzif dropped us at the beach and said she'd be back in two hours. Nina and I each settled into our chairs, wearing our swimsuits, with a cooler full of snacks between us.

"So you haven't heard from Jai at all?" Nina asked, pulling her sunglasses down over her nose.

"Nope," I said as I smoothed sunblock onto my pale shoulders.

"Has he liked any of your Relay posts?"

"Also a no."

"And you haven't seen him at any events?"

"We just got back last night, so no. At this point I'm dreading running into him at the next event, though." I frowned. "I know I have to stop obsessing about this. He just . . . I guess he didn't actually like me at all. I need to dust myself off and move on."

"While I applaud you being such a brave little toaster, you might be writing the end too fast, Sam. It is summer. You just got back from a vacay—maybe *he's* on a trip."

"Yeah, with Amara," I grumbled as I shook the sand from the bottom of my water bottle.

"Sam!" Nina said with a laugh. "Jai's our age—it's not like he's going on a romantic getaway with somebody. All I was saying was that nothing's decided for sure."

"Also, why am I a toaster?" I asked her. "Why not a brave little grill, or a nice sauté pan? My culinary skills extend way beyond toasting."

"It was a movie, maniac. My dad makes me watch all this animated stuff from when he was a kid." Nina rolled her eyes. "Try sitting through *The Great Mouse Detective*."

"I'm okay, thanks." I sighed and leaned back in my chair. "Anyway, enough about Jai."

"So what else did I miss while I was away?" Nina asked, opening the cooler between our feet to take out some of the yummy beach snacks I'd packed.

"Your trip lasted forever," I said. "Mostly you missed out on a huge chunk of the pugs' young lives."

"I *was* sad not to see Pepper and Jack," Nina said. "But you were good about sending me real-time text updates on them. Of course, they're also dominating my Relay feed. How did that happen, anyway? I mean, they're super cute, but you used to have like eleven followers."

"It started with Allie's post!" I said. "And Jai posted and

tagged the pugs a bunch, too, and he has a lot of followers," I added.

"We're back to Jai, huh?" Nina waggled her eyebrows at me and I threw my T-shirt at her. "Sam, quit—that's sandy. Anyway, you teased me when I had a crush on Michael Carlson last year."

"That's because Michael Carlson isn't worthy of you," I pointed out. "I had language arts with him this year and he asked me how to spell *citrus*. Unlike me, *you* are good at everything. You need a boyfriend who's on your level."

"Not true! I mean, I agree with the on-my-level part, but I'm not good at everything."

"Math, history, writing, Spanish . . ." I ticked off each item on my fingers.

"School all counts as one thing," Nina said.

"It had better not, or my lack of math ability will cancel out my being good at English. Also, you're good at improv comedy . . ."

"Stop." Nina playfully swatted my arm. "You'll give me a big head."

"Too late."

She swatted my arm again. "Ha ha. Well, speaking of improv, are you ready for the retreat on Monday?"

"When I think about it my stomach clenches and I kind of want to throw up."

"That's normal, but you're going to rock it."

"If you say so."

"I do say so." Nina leaned back in her chair and stretched, pointing her toes with a happy sigh. "This is awesome. Don't you feel better just being here? Is there any problem in the world that a day at the beach can't fix?"

I looked over at her. "Sunburn?"

She sat up with an exaggerated frown, but then grinned and threw *her* T-shirt at me. "I guess you got me there."

16

Runaway Pugs

It all started with an unusually large lizard. There are a lot of tiny lizards running around South Florida, and Jack, in particular, had a fondness for chasing after them whenever he spotted one on our porch.

So, yes, I knew Jack was interested in lizards. But what I didn't know was that he was going to spot one in the middle of dinner service at the Williams-Pittman Advertising company party, bust through the (apparently broken) door of the pugs' travel crate, take off after that lizard, and end up tripping a waiter who was carrying a tray full of pasta primavera entrées.

Pepper took off after Jack, so then there were two small pugs running wild through the tented party. Someone even screamed. Of course, as soon as I realized what was happening, I started running after the pugs, and then Dad took off after me, still holding a piping bag full of icing, but squeezing it in his excitement, so long threads of purple icing were trailing behind him.

The DJ—Dr. Jams hadn't been hired for this event, thankfully—stopped playing music, so before long, everyone was staring. I was trying very hard to catch Jack, but it turns out dogs are *fast* when they run full-out. Finally, Mom had the idea to use food to catch the pups, and she managed to get Jack's attention with a handful of leftover steak crostini appetizers. It worked. Jack approached Mom, and Pepper joined in, and soon the pugs were eating out of her hand. Then I snuck up and grabbed Jack, and Dad grabbed Pepper.

"Sorry, folks!" Dad said to the guests in a loud but nervous voice as he carried Pepper and I carried Jack back toward the kitchen, Mom marching ahead of us.

"Dogs near the food prep area, Melissa?" a woman asked in an annoyed voice.

I turned around to see a woman in a suit approaching Mom with a frown. I recognized the woman as Patty, the manager of the property where the event was being held. I could tell by Mom's face that I was in big trouble. Dad told me to take the pups to the van and wait with them, since the crate was obviously broken and we couldn't risk them getting out again, not at this party.

It was a long wait with the puppies. Mom and Dad had to finish the rest of the dinner, and then do cleanup. I wished Ollie were there to keep me company, but he had been shipped off to Colin's house. I played with the pugs until they got tired and then they curled up on the back seat beside me and fell asleep. I wished I were a little older so I could drive, or my parents would at least let me take an Uber home, though I wondered if Ubers usually allowed pets.

Finally, Mom and Dad came back to the van, heads down.

"What happened?" I asked them, my stomach twisting.

"Patty wasn't happy," Mom said. "But I convinced her this was a one-time thing since I needed your help and the dogs were too little to be left alone. But this has to be the last event for those two."

I nodded, my throat tight. "Are you mad at me?" I asked.

Dad and Mom both looked surprised. "You didn't do anything wrong, Sam," Dad said. "We let you bring the dogs to the event."

"And it's not your fault the crate broke," Mom added.

"I'll stay back home with Pepper and Jack for the next event," I said sadly. "I love cooking—and helping. But until they're old enough . . ."

"Thanks, kid. That's probably what we're going to have to do," Dad said.

When we got home, I saw a bunch of notifications on my Relay account. Someone at the party had made a video of Jack and Pepper's wild lizard chase and set it to funny music. They'd posted it with the tag #pugtwinsWPB so I was seeing all the likes and comments. And there were already 812 likes. The post was going viral. I wanted to chuckle watching the video, but I still remembered the look on Mom's face when Patty was chewing her out.

I wondered who had made the video, but then I couldn't wonder for long. I had to take the pugs out, get ready for bed, and make plans to go to the pet store in the morning to get a new travel crate.

One with a much stronger door, of course.

17

No . . .

The next morning, Dad took Ollie to the pet store to buy a new crate. Mom was in the kitchen, and I was sitting in the living room playing with the pugs.

Jack was the first to notice the feet shuffling back and forth in front of our gate. It was locked, so the person might have knocked, but we wouldn't have heard it. We used to have an electronic doorbell out there, but it got ruined in the last big hurricane.

Jack started barking. Mom dried her hands on a dish towel and went out onto the porch to investigate.

"Maybe it's a delivery," she said, even though all the delivery people in our neighborhood knew to just leave the package right outside the gate.

I picked up Jack and tried to calm him down. Pepper had started barking because he was, so I scooped her up, too.

I was holding both of them when Mom called my name. Her voice sounded funny.

I went out to the porch. Mom was facing a blonde girl I didn't know. She looked like she was probably in high school.

"This is Karen," Mom said. "She says the pugs were meant to be delivered to her."

I felt everything stop when Mom said those words. It seemed like the fountain in the lake outside our town house stopped gurgling, the hum of the birds and the insects disappeared. I felt frozen, too, like I couldn't speak or move. How? How could this happen now? Now, when I loved them so much . . . I couldn't imagine possibly letting them go now. I tightened my hold on the pups and took a step backward.

"I'm real sorry for the mix-up and all," the girl—Karen—said.

As if any sort of *sorry* could possibly cover what had happened.

"You can't," I managed to say. "You can't take them." I held the pugs even closer. Jack licked my face. Pepper blinked at Karen, curious. Did the pugs know Karen? They didn't seem to.

"Sam," Mom chided me. I knew I wasn't being polite. But Mom looked upset, too. Her face was tight and her voice still sounded weird. "Maybe you could come inside for a few minutes and we could talk some more about this," Mom told Karen.

"Oh. Okay." Karen sounded surprised. Did she think we were just going to hand our dogs over right there on the porch after she'd said ten words to us? I looked at her, at her winged black eyeliner, and what I decided was a smug look on her face. I didn't think I'd ever hated anyone before that moment. Mom would probably say *hate* was too strong a word. I took a deep breath and tried to keep calm.

Karen followed us inside, and she and Mom went into the kitchen. I put the pugs in the living room, leaving them with toys. Then I hurried into the kitchen. Mom was sitting at the

171

kitchen table and I sat beside her. Karen sat on the edge of a chair, like she didn't plan to stay long.

"Karen, this is my daughter, Sam," Mom explained, gesturing to me. "She's the one who found the dogs, and she's been working hard taking care of them . . ."

"Oh, thank you!" Karen interrupted Mom.

"That's not what I was getting at," Mom said, a little sharply. "What I was going to say was, perhaps you wouldn't mind telling Sam the story you started to tell me outside? About your . . . boyfriend, was it?" she prompted.

Karen nodded and looked at me. "Right, so I was telling your mom here that my BF bought these pugs for me, as a gift, you know—it was a late birthday present, actually. Anyhow, I live over in the north complex? You know, just up the road—so we've got the same type of porch that you all do. Our roofs are darker in color, though, which I tried to tell Chris—my BF—but he never listens, you know."

"So how did he end up leaving the dogs on our porch?" I asked.

Karen gave a small laugh. "Well, he got the address mixed around. He must have mixed up the numbers somehow and accidentally left the dogs here."

Mom frowned. "Okay, Karen, I see what you're saying," she began. "But I have to say I just don't understand how you're only coming to ask about the dogs now. We've had them for over a month. How did it take you this long to realize your boyfriend had left them in the wrong place?"

"And why would he just leave them in a box in the hot sun?" I added, but Mom shook her head at me. I didn't understand why we were being careful of this Karen person's feelings but I shut my mouth, at least for the time being.

"We've both been traveling," Karen explained. "My boyfriend's family lives in Venezuela, so he's been down there."

"Oh," I said, even though that didn't really explain things. I glanced at Mom, and I was glad she looked as uncertain as I felt.

"Karen, this is all very sudden," Mom said, "and I have to say I'm still not completely satisfied about why it's taken so long. I'd also feel more comfortable making any final decisions with my husband here, and quite frankly your parents. This is a family matter, you understand. We've taken the dogs to the vet; it's been an investment . . ."

"Thank you for doing all that . . . ," Karen said.

Mom put her hand up. "Of course. But listen, can you come back later? My husband will be here, and we can discuss this further. I think we'd all feel better if we met your parents as well, as I mentioned."

Karen's face seemed to harden. "Well, they're still traveling."

"Perhaps they could FaceTime or Skype into our meeting, then." This was the all-business side of Mom, the one who negotiated with stubborn clients. I'd never admired or loved her more. Even with my heart pounding, I could appreciate how great she was being. The only thing that would be greater would be if she said, *The dogs are ours, get out.* But what if Karen really was telling the truth? Would she ever let it go, in that case? What if she really did come back with her parents?

"I can't come later, but Tuesday might work. I guess I'll check with my parents," Karen was saying to Mom.

Mom rose, clearly signaling that it was time for Karen to leave. She handed Karen a Calloway's Creations business card. "Give me a call. Let us know for certain about Tuesday," she told her.

Karen stood up, and followed Mom out of the house. I heard Mom lock the gate behind Karen when she left.

I dashed back into the living room to find Pepper and Jack happily playing with their squeaky toys. I sat down and hugged them both close to me, feeling like I was going to cry.

When Mom came back inside, she looked at me with the saddest expression on her face. "Oh, Sam—I'm so sorry," she said.

I looked up at her. Somewhere along the line she must have decided that the pugs could stay with us after all. But then it occurred to me that she wouldn't be saying she was sorry unless she believed the dogs might actually belong to Karen.

"But—no—you thought it, too—I know you did!" I cried. "Karen's story stinks! Something's not right . . ."

Mom frowned and sat down beside me on the floor. "Something does have an odor, but the thing is, Sam, I really can't imagine why someone would want to concoct a story like that. As strange as Karen's story is, it's really even stranger that she would make one up to come to our door and take our dogs. The north complex buildings *do* look just like the ones in ours," she added.

"Yes, but how do you explain this 'BF' of hers just leaving the dogs here? And never checking on what happened after?"

While Karen had been here, I'd started to feel like Mom and Dad were going to fix this. But now, with Mom saying what she was saying, I wasn't so sure. I felt hot tears start to fall down my cheeks.

"It's not fair." I held Jack and Pepper up closer to my chest and cried on their fur. They stared up at me, their dark eyes serious and sad.

"I know, sweetie. I know. Look, we're going to insist on meeting her parents, at least virtually, and we're also going to ask about where her boyfriend got the pugs—for a receipt or papers from a shelter or something. But, sweetheart, if they have all that, you have to get ready . . ."

"No!" I wailed and rocked back and forth with the puppies.

Ollie opened the door, and he and Dad walked in with the new crate. They took one look at me and Mom and knew something was wrong.

"What's happening?" Ollie asked, looking at me, his blue eyes huge in his face.

"Melissa?" Dad asked, looking at Mom.

Quickly, Mom explained what had happened with Karen. Ollie started shaking his head, fast. "No!" he burst out, sounding angry. He marched over to me and grabbed Pepper from my arms. "No one's taking them!" He ran upstairs with Pepper and slammed his door.

Then I heard the worst sound I'd ever heard in my life: my little brother, who hardly ever showed any emotion at all, sobbing his heart out.

I looked at Mom and Dad, but they shook their heads helplessly. Tuesday. Karen would be back on Tuesday. I hugged Jack to my chest. I couldn't imagine handing him over to a stranger in a couple of days, and never seeing him again. I couldn't imagine it, and I didn't want to.

18

Animal Summer

With the arrival of Karen, and the fear of losing the puppies to her, I'd completely forgotten that the next day was one I had been dreading: the improv comedy retreat.

"I can't go," I told Nina on the phone.

"You have to," she said. "I know you're upset, and I get it—I would be, too. But, Sam, I think a distraction is exactly what you need right now. What are you going to do, sit at home and obsess over this Karen person coming on Tuesday?"

Nina had a point there, and she knew it, so eventually she wore me down. Soon enough, it was Monday and I was sitting in the back seat of her dad's car on the way to the high school, where the retreat was being held.

"Stop fidgeting," Nina told me from the front seat.

"How can you see what I'm doing?"

"In the rearview mirror."

"Give me a break! I'm kind of stressed out right now. And besides, you're dragging me to this thing where I probably have to go up on a stage of some kind . . ."

"Not probably. Definitely."

"Seriously?!" I cried.

"You *just* said . . ."

"Girls, girls—come on, it's summer, time to be relaxed and not worry about anything!" Mr. Katzif piped up. Nina's dad is a college professor, so he's off in the summer, too.

"*D-ad*," Nina said. "Sam *is* worried about that girl who said the dogs belong to her. I told you."

"Sorry, Sam," Mr. Katzif said.

"It's okay," I said glumly. I was already regretting coming. I was going to be miserable wherever I was, but at least at home

I could have distracted myself with something non-scary, like Netflix.

"You're going to have a good time at the retreat—I promise. It'll be a great time to bond with the group before the school year starts," Nina was telling me.

"I still haven't said yes to joining the improv group," I told her. That was Nina's ultimate mission in getting me to come.

"Like you have a choice," Nina muttered.

"Hey!"

"Girls!" Mr. Katzif repeated.

Luckily, he'd just pulled into a parking space at the high school, so we could at least keep bickering without a referee getting in the way.

I followed Nina into the back entrance to the school and through the dark hallways until we reached the auditorium. A whole bunch of kids were already there, sitting in a rough circle on the stage. I knew most of them by sight, but there was no one—except Nina—who I knew very well. I realized that I'd been expecting to see Gaby Martin, who used to eat lunch with me and Nina sometimes, but I'd forgotten that her family had gone to Dallas for the whole summer. Just then, it felt like one more thing going wrong and I felt like crying again. It wasn't going to take much today to push me over the edge. Every time I closed my eyes I saw Pepper and Jack and their sweet little faces . . . and I relived the moment of walking outside our house and finding Karen standing there.

Nina and I sat in the circle. The kids waved at both of us, and asked how our summers were going. And then they all started talking about the shows they'd done last year, and funny stories from them, until the team's advisor, Ms. Miller, came in and said they were going to start things off by doing a round of Family Portrait.

"Groups of five," Ms. Miller added, and everybody started getting in groups. I sat there, confused, not knowing what to do. I looked around and it seemed like the big group had, in seconds, turned into five perfect groups of five—with one random leftover: me.

Suddenly I felt Nina pulling my arm, and I tried not to let my relief show too much as she said, "Join our group."

Ms. Miller walked around and handed someone in each group a small slip of paper. Nina grabbed our piece of paper, and everyone huddled up to read the words. I couldn't quite see what the paper said, but then Nina whispered "Circus performers" in my ear, which was just as good as no information because I had no idea what those words meant in this context.

Before I knew it, Nina was sitting on the floor, pretending to lick her own hand; Marshall Goodwin was standing next to her waving his arms around; Lora Barton seemed to be walking on an invisible balance beam; and the Carter twins had joined arms. I was frozen in confusion, again.

"Do something like you're in the circus," Nina told me as Ms. Miller yelled out for everyone in our group to freeze.

The rest of the group members were staring at us—I mean, at me, because I was just standing there like a fool.

"Any guesses?" Ms. Miller asked the other kids not in our group.

"Playground?" someone said, and Ms. Miller shook her head.

"What's she doing?" a girl I didn't know was pointing at me and asking.

"Carnival—or circus?" someone called out.

"Yep, that's it," Ms. Miller. "Good job, you guys—now team two!"

I moved to stand beside Nina as everyone came out of their poses. I felt so stupid for just standing there.

"How was I supposed to know how to do that?" I muttered.

"I'm sorry, I should have prepped you better. I thought you'd just kind of go with it," Nina whispered back. "You'll get the next one—just hang in there, okay?"

"I told you I wouldn't be any good . . ."

"Sam, stop—just give it a chance, will you? We've been here ten minutes!" she hissed in my ear.

I watched the next group go, feeling raw. Everyone participated; no one just froze like I had. I felt my face heat up and my stomach felt sick. I couldn't do this. I walked off the stage, and then I started running. I ran blindly down the dark hallways until I finally found a door labeled GIRLS. I pushed open the door, hurtled inside, and was finally able to let go of the tears that had been threatening ever since I'd gotten stuck onstage. I sat on the floor and hugged my knees. No wonder I stuck to cooking—that was something I was good at, something I understood. I definitely blamed Nina for dragging me here. Everyone else in this group knew what they were doing, knew the language Ms. Miller was speaking. How could Nina even think that I could handle this right now?

Just then, Nina burst into the bathroom. "Sam! Thank goodness I finally found you—are you okay? Oh no—have you been crying?"

I wiped at my eyes with the back of my hand and hung my head. "Yeah."

"I can text my dad and he can come pick you up. Or both of us—I can go with you."

"No, Nina, you're the captain, you're not missing this. Besides, you've been looking forward to this for a month."

"If you go, I go," she said, hands on her hips. I could tell she was serious.

I looked up at her. "Nina, I can't go back in there. I just . . . ran away, like . . ." Suddenly I realized who I'd just acted like. "Like Ollie did."

At that moment it was so clear. I'd just done the exact same thing Ollie had done when I called him a slug. I'd felt stupid and useless, and maybe so had he. After all, I didn't give him a chance to show that he could help, not really. He ruined one mushroom and I yelled at him.

Nina hadn't done that with me. She'd just said *you'll get the next one*. Now she was vowing to leave, to miss something she loved, all so she could take care of me.

I'd had one taste of being the odd one out, and it had left me crying on the bathroom floor. I knew that part of it was Karen and the pugs, but I still felt guilty about how I'd treated Ollie. And then when Jai had pointed it out to me, I'd yelled at him, too.

I grabbed on to the sink and pulled myself up. I couldn't do anything about Karen and the pugs, or Jai, or Ollie right now. But there was one thing I could do. I could actually try something new, and not run away the first time it got hard.

"I'm going to give it another try," I told Nina. "I think I need to."

"Okay, if you're sure," Nina said, looking wary. I gave her my best game face, and then followed her back down the hall to the theater.

The next improv game was already underway when we got there. Nina and I sat on the side of the stage and she whispered in my ear. "This game is called the Dating Game. I know it sounds weird, but it's actually really fun to play. Lilah there is the main contestant—she's the only one who doesn't know what character the three guys are playing. She asks each of them the same three questions, and based on how they answer and play their characters, she has to guess who they are."

Nina and I watched, and Lilah guessed that the boys had been playing Kanye West, Joey from *Friends*, and Superman.

"The first two were right—but Jon was Mr. Incredible, not Superman," Ms. Miller said.

"That's pretty close," I said, surprised that I'd gotten sort of sucked into watching the game.

Nina looked at me. "The next round's got three girls—you want to draw a slip and play?"

I could feel my heartbeat in my ears, but I nodded. Nina ran over to Ms. Miller, then came back with the hat. I felt like everyone was staring at me again as I stood up, reached in, and pulled out a slip of paper. I looked down at the paper in my hand. It said: ANIMAL FROM THE MUPPETS.

Maybe I'd pretended to be brave too soon.

Nina and Lindsey drew their characters from the hat. A boy named Travis, who was going to guess who we were, left the stage area. Nina, Lindsey, and I each announced our characters to the rest of the group. Nina was Barbie, and Lindsey was Mrs. Claus.

I wondered how lame it would look if I asked to draw another name. From what Nina had told me, pretty lame. She says that improvisational comedy is all about saying yes. You're always just supposed to go for it, always try.

So, when I spotted a snare drum backstage, I ran to get it.

Travis came out then and sat in his chair, and we three girls took ours.

"Okay, contestant number one," Travis began. "Describe your perfect day."

Nina put on a high-pitched voice and said, "We go for a

drive in my dream car, and then go sit near some plastic food. Then I go shopping for some high heels!"

Lindsey, aka Mrs. Claus, described a snowy Christmas day after all the gifts had been unwrapped, with some hot cocoa and a room full of happy elves.

Then it was my turn. My heart was pounding. I felt myself start to freeze, but I fought it. I couldn't bear the thought of just sitting there, washing out completely like I'd done in the first exercise. So I started to do the sort of pant/growl combo I remembered the Muppet Animal doing. Then I banged my fists on the snare drum. "Animal drum!" I yelled, knowing I looked ridiculous but deciding not to care. "All day Animal DRUM!" I got up on the chair in a crouch and kept banging. "Drummmmmmmm!"

And then the most amazing thing happened. I realized that people were laughing. Like, really, really laughing. At me, sure. But not in a mean way. In a way that made me smile and then laugh myself.

The rest of the day got a lot easier after that—in fact, it started to be kind of fun. Getting those laughs had felt so good. It wasn't the same as someone complimenting food I'd cooked, but still really great. The best part was, I'd gone for a long while without worrying about losing the pugs.

"I knew that you'd rock at this," Nina said as we walked to her dad's car afterward.

"Well, that made one of us. But I really did not suck, huh? At least not after the first game."

"That was my fault—I should have prepped you better," Nina said. "Once you knew the drill, you killed it. I think your Animal got more laughs than anything else today."

"This has been my summer of animals." I turned to her, growing serious. "I'm not going to give up Pepper and Jack without a fight," I told her.

"I know. And I'll help you," she vowed.

I opened the door when I got home and called Ollie's name. Neither our parents' car nor the catering van was parked outside. I was hoping my little brother was home, though. Mom usually only left him alone for really short periods of time. Maybe she'd gone to the grocery store again. She did practically live there.

Ollie came downstairs from his room. "Were you yelling?" he asked. Pepper was tucked under his arm, and Jack was at his heels.

I nodded. "I was. Hey, do you have a sec? I wanted to talk to you a little."

He gave me a wary look. "I don't want to talk about that Karen person."

"No, I'm with you on that. But this is actually about you and me."

"Okay." He sat down on the step he'd been standing on, which left me awkwardly standing in front of the stairs. Pepper sat down beside him, but Jack came over to me. I grabbed one of the kitchen chairs and dragged it over. I sat cross-legged and picked up Jack and settled him in my lap.

I took a deep breath. "Okay, so I figured out that I owe you an apology, Ollie. And I'm sorry it's so late, but I was . . . it just took me a little bit to realize it. Anyway, I'm sorry about what I said, and how I acted, the night you . . . you know, the night you got upset. When you ran away from us . . . from me."

"Yeah, I remember."

"Well, anyway, I shouldn't have called you a slug. That was mean. I should have realized that cooking's not your thing. Or maybe . . ." I trailed off. I thought about how that morning I hadn't thought comedy was my "thing"—but then I'd had a blast. "Ollie, is it possible that you're maybe just a *little* bit interested in cooking?"

He was giving me a strange look that I couldn't read. "Cooking is your thing," he finally said.

"Ollie, cooking is a *Calloway* thing. What if you just tried a fun and easy recipe, to see how you liked it? No pressure?"

Again, he paused, scratching Pepper behind her ears. "Would you show me?"

I nodded. "I'd love to. I have a book of recipes I've been wanting to try—maybe you could look at it and help me pick one?"

Ollie nodded. "Okay."

The look on Mom's face when she came home and found us both in the kitchen making dinner was completely priceless.

19

Backup

"Karen called and she *is* coming tomorrow. With her mother," Mom told me as we were washing the dishes.

I almost dropped the glass I was drying.

"Okay," I heard myself say. But it wasn't okay. It was the farthest possible distance from okay.

After dinner, I went upstairs with Jack, and Ollie took Pepper to his room. Mom didn't say anything about bringing the pugs upstairs. Which made me more worried than anything. She would be a stickler for the rules if she thought the dogs were staying.

My stomach was clenched so tightly I was beginning to regret eating dinner.

I got a text from Nina saying to meet her on Relay chat, so I logged on. It felt good to see her face. I felt at least 7 percent better right away.

"So, what time is this Karen coming tomorrow?" she asked. "I'll come for moral support."

"Really?"

"Of course, dummy. I'm not letting you deal with this without your BFF."

I smiled, relieved. "Thanks, Nina. I mean it. I don't even know how I'm going to get through this if she takes them . . ."

"It's not gonna happen. I feel like your mom is gonna break bad on this woman tomorrow—that's actually the main reason I want to be there. I want to witness it."

I couldn't help but laugh. "They're coming at twelve thirty. But come over early."

"I will. We have to observe everything that she does and says. It could come up later in court."

"Nina, I don't think my parents are prepared to get a lawyer over the pugs."

Nina shrugged. "My dad's fraternity friend from UF is a lawyer. Maybe Dad can call him."

"Yeah, maybe. I guess ask him. Man, this is all so crazy. I just keep coming back to how weird it all is. Who doesn't realize they didn't get the *dogs* they were supposed to get as a present for more than a month?"

"We'll figure it out, Sammy. Seriously. Maybe you should try to get some sleep?"

"Fat chance," I said as I scratched Jack's belly.

"Well, I'll stay on with you," Nina said with a yawn. I felt a pang of guilt. Just because I couldn't sleep was no reason my best friend shouldn't.

"No, I think I am getting a little tired after all. I'm going to try to sleep," I lied.

"Okay, if you're sure," Nina said with another yawn.

"I'm sure. Night, Nina," I said.

"Night, Sammy."

When Nina was gone, I scrolled through Relay, looking for more distractions. Then I saw a familiar face in my friends list, and I realized there was one more thing I could do tonight. Even if it was a long shot, at least I'd be taking action. It took a long time to compose the perfect message, but I wasn't sleeping anyway.

Hi Jai,

You might not even want to read this message, which I would understand, but I wanted to tell you that I'm sorry. I realize now that it was my fault—our fight, I mean. I was wrong to get so defensive. Maybe on some level I knew that you had a point. I did this really scary new thing today, and because of it I had this moment where I understood Ollie better. So he and I had a pretty good talk tonight (well, I did most of the talking, but that's my brother).

Anyway, I'm sorry for how things went between us that night.

Also, something just happened. Someone came forward yesterday, claiming that the pugs are hers. Her story doesn't totally make sense, but she's coming back tomorrow, and I'm so afraid this is the last night I'll have with Pepper and Jack.

So that's where I am right now and I felt like I had to tell you.

Sincerely,

Sam

Just a few minutes later I got a notification ping from Relay. I had a new direct message. I took a deep breath and closed my eyes. Maybe I shouldn't open it tonight. What if it was just Jai saying that he never wanted to talk to me again? But waiting wouldn't change what was in the message, and the suspense was pretty torturous. I exhaled, opened my eyes, and read the message.

Dear Sam,

I'm so glad you sent this, but I'm so, so sorry to hear that someone came forward about Pepper and Jack. I can't believe it's happening now, after all this time. I also have to tell you, though, that I hope you can forgive me for being such a know-it-all jerk.

I felt so bad after our fight that it got me thinking. I ended up calling my mom, and we talked, like really talked—for the first time in a long time. It was weirdly easier over the phone. I found out I was wrong about a lot of things. I thought she wanted me to go away so she could be alone with Nate, my new stepdad. But actually she thought *I* was going because I felt left out or was mad at her. So maybe I'm not as great at communicating as I thought I was.

I actually decided after a lot of soul-searching to stay in Florida with my dad for the rest of the year. Once Mom and I talked it out, I realized that she and Nate are on kind of shaky ground, although I think she loves him. I think she needs some more time and space, and maybe I need to give my dad more of a shot.

I was such a big talker to you about being sensitive to what your brother needs but I wasn't doing the same thing for my own father. After being here with him this summer

I realized he doesn't really pick up on hints—you have to ask him things outright. I think the way Mom was trying to get him to invite me for the summer just never registered with him. I'm wondering now if we'd just *asked* maybe everything would have been different. Dad was so great this summer. He really surprised me—he even agreed to let me bring my best friend, Dipper, down here for the rest of the year!

I really hope that Dipper can meet Pepper and Jack. If there's anything I can do, or if you just want to vent about it, I'm here.

—Jai

Right below his name, Jai had also typed in his phone number. I hesitated for all of thirty seconds before sending him a text.

Got your message. So glad u don't hate me.

Hey! Glad u don't hate me either. But I'm sorry again about the pups ☹

I'm so afraid about tomorrow. Can't sleep.

Now I can't either. Will stay up with you. Can you FaceTime?

Yes.

I answered the FaceTime call and almost cried with relief when I saw Jai's face. Seeing him right now made a terrible night just a little less terrible.

"So tell me about this person and everything that happened," he said, so I did.

Jai listened sympathetically, and after a while, I finally started to feel sleepy. We said good night and I lay down and closed my eyes.

I woke up still clutching my phone, with Jack snoring beside me. I looked at the time: 6:47 in the morning. I didn't even try to go back to sleep. I decided to go downstairs and make some cocoa.

But someone was already in the kitchen making it: my aunt Maddie!

"What are you doing here?" I asked Maddie. "Not that I'm not glad . . ."

She put up a hand. "Say no more. Let's just say when my big

sister calls me crying at one o'clock in the morning, I call in sick to work and get in the car."

I turned around then and spotted Mom sitting at the kitchen table. "Wait, *you* were crying? I didn't even think you liked . . ."

"I like them fine. But I was crying because I know how much you and Ollie *love* them."

And then *I* started crying, and Mom and Maddie enfolded me in a big hug. Even though I was afraid, I realized that I'd gotten through the night with help from Nina and, unexpectedly, Jai. And now Maddie was here, too, thanks to Mom.

I stepped out of the hug, finally, wiping away tears. This was all a terrible mess, but it sure was good to have backup.

20

Karen's Back

"Nina will be here at noon," I told Mom as I helped her clear the breakfast dishes.

"Wait, why is Nina coming?" Mom asked. "Sam, this is a family situation."

I felt my chin rise a notch as I prepared to argue. "First, Nina *is* family. And second, I really need her here for this. *You* have Maddie here," I added.

Mom frowned but nodded. "All right."

Nina knocked on the door at eleven forty-five. "I didn't want to be late," she said, marching into the living room. "So, listen,

I've been thinking, we should let this Karen person do all the talking. Don't give her any information."

Dad snorted from where he sat on the sofa, reading the paper. "Been reading Sherlock Holmes again, Nina?"

Nina straightened her shoulders. "I'll have you know, Mr. Calloway, that I am the president of our school's forensic science club."

I looked at her in confusion but didn't rat her out. "I've been sort of planning to start one," she said in my ear. "Which would naturally make me the president."

I smiled. I wondered if it would be my last smile of the day.

Finally, at twelve thirty on the dot, Karen knocked on our door. Mom had insisted we leave the gate unlocked, over my protests.

Karen was alone—which seemed like a good start. Mom had asked her to produce some sort of parent. But then again, she had said they were "traveling."

"Hello, Karen," Mom said, taking the lead as Karen walked inside. "This is my husband, Dan. And you remember my daughter, Sam. This is her best friend, Nina." Karen made a face, briefly, at that part, but she stepped forward and shook Dad's hand.

"And I'm Maddie, the aunt," Maddie announced, not waiting for an introduction. Ollie had refused to come out of his room, which made it a perfect place for the puppies to stay, away from the meeting.

We all sat down in the living room.

"I'd like to hear more about what happened in May, with the pugs," Dad said to her without any lead-up. Mom gestured to an empty chair and Karen sat.

"Yeah, she acted like she needed to run all this by you," Karen said, pointing at my mother. I saw Maddie put a hand on Mom's arm as though to restrain her. This girl was off to a rough start today with Mom. I was glad. The worse she acted, I figured, the less likely it would be that she would leave here with my dogs. "Where are the dogs, by the way?"

"Let's get back to what happened in May," Dad repeated. I liked the way he kept repeating "in May"—since it was late June now, and where the heck had she been all this time if they really were her dogs?

"I kind of love your dad," Nina hissed in my ear.

"Me too," I whispered back.

"Well, as I said the last time I was here, it was just a mix-up," Karen replied. "My boyfriend got me the dogs as a gift, and he delivered them to the wrong address. I live over in the north complex. He got the numbers mixed up."

"Yes, I see," Dad said. "But that still doesn't explain the very long delay in coming to claim them."

"Both my boyfriend and I were traveling," Karen said, sounding a little bit snippy. "Not together, but we were both away. I already explained all this before."

"If you weren't going to be home, why was your boyfriend bringing a box of dogs to you *at* your home?" Maddie asked.

It was a good question. Go Aunt Maddie!

Karen frowned. "My trip was unexpected. Look, I don't want to make a big thing of this, so you can just give me the pugs and . . ."

"Karen, you keep mentioning the fact that you 'already explained' things the last time we met," Mom said. "Well, I also explained something to you the last time, remember?

I asked you to bring at least one of your parents, either in person or via Skype or FaceTime. I'm not going to just turn these animals over to someone your age."

Yay, Mom!

Karen stood up. "My parents are in the military, so I can't just *Skype* with them at the drop of a hat. But I'll get them to record a video message, if that's what you need before doing the right thing. And I'll also bring a copy of the dogs' pedigree papers, and anything else that would be needed—legally—to claim them. I won't be staying. I'll call you after I get the video, and everything."

I sagged against Nina as Karen walked out of our house. "What a horrible girl! I feel like she was threatening us," Mom said.

"That's because she was," Maddie said with a frown.

"What's with the mysterious parents both suddenly being in the military?" Dad asked. "Is this the first she's mentioned that?"

Both Mom and I nodded.

"Well, we can analyze it all in detail. I've got it all recorded," Nina said, holding up her phone.

"Nina!" Mom said, sounding scandalized.

But Maddie just grinned at her and said, "Good job, Nina!"

21

Calloway-Katzif-Jambagi Investigations, Inc.

After Karen left, Nina suggested that she and I go out for Starbucks, and then I could sleep over at her house that night. She told my parents it would be good for me to get out a little, and they agreed. But the real reason for the invitation, Nina explained to me in a whisper, was to give us time to work on "the case."

So I said goodbye to my parents and Ollie, hugged Pepper and Jack extra tight, and packed a small bag. Nina's dad picked us up and drove us to Starbucks.

In the car, I saw I had a bunch of texts from Jai, so I asked him if he could meet us at Starbucks, too. He said he'd be there soon.

Nina's dad dropped us off and Nina and I grabbed a table. Right away Nina started unpacking her laptop, a notebook, and a fresh pack of twenty-four different-color gel pens. If only this situation were fixable with extreme color-coding, I reflected as Jai walked in.

I thought it would be awkward to see him after all this time, but it wasn't at all.

"Hey," I said, smiling, and he smiled back.

I was glad he was here, and even more glad that he was game to try to help us figure out what Karen was up to.

Jai volunteered to get us our Frappuccinos, and soon we were all settled at the table with our drinks.

"So," I began, "I think the real question here is: Why is this Karen girl doing this? Why does she want Pepper and Jack?"

I frowned. Saying their names out loud in the same sentence as Karen's name made me feel kind of sick.

"I agree," Nina said, nodding. "I met her at Sam's house,"

she explained to Jai. "And she does *not* seem like the warm fuzzy type. I mean, they're super cute pugs, but that doesn't seem like enough of a reason. She seems like she wants *something*, though."

"Does she want to sell them?" Jai wondered out loud. "I mean, if it's not because she saw them and fell in love . . . wait!" Jai put both palms flat on the table, hard enough to move my Frappuccino a couple of inches. "Sorry, but I just had a thought. Before we figure out why she wants them, I think we need to figure out *how* she knows about them. I mean, if we assume she's lying about the whole present-from-her-boyfriend thing."

I nodded. "That is a good point. I hadn't even thought . . . I mean, she could have seen them online. On Relay—they do have a lot of followers."

"So we go through the follower list," Nina said, fingers hovering above her laptop's keyboard.

"Although people don't always use their actual pictures—or their real names—for their Relay accounts," I said with a frown.

"And I don't even know what she looks like," Jai added.

"I have a picture!" Nina said, and pulled it up on her phone. "I snuck a picture while she was there today."

"You are such a spy!" I told Nina, who grinned.

"Well, since Nina's got a pic, let's do an image search," Jai suggested.

I stared down at Nina's phone and the image of Karen sitting there on my sofa. "Looking at this picture, I feel like there's something familiar about her," I said, but I couldn't place it.

"Good idea," Nina was saying to Jai. "Let me just email myself this picture and we'll search."

Nina hit the keys on her laptop with even more than her usual gusto. A few seconds later she announced, "Well, crap."

"What did you find?" Jai asked.

Nina frowned and began to read, *"Best guess for this image: girl. A girl is a young female human . . .* Should I go on?"

"No, it didn't work, we get the picture. No pun intended," I added glumly.

"Maybe this photo could be enhanced somehow and we could do another search," Nina said. I could tell she was trying to sound positive, but also that she was faking the sound of confidence. "What's her last name?"

"I don't think she ever said it. But we should definitely ask next time she comes over."

"Let's start with Relay," Jai said, sitting up straighter in his chair. "If we assume she saw the pugs on there and decided she wanted them, then she's on there, too."

"Do you think she wants to take over their social media account? For the likes and follows?" Nina asked.

This time I sat up straighter in my seat. "What do you mean?"

"Well, Pepper and Jack could be on their way to becoming celebrity pugs," Nina said. "Look at Doug the Pug. Or that celebrity dachshund—Crusoe. My cousin always sends me those videos. Those are both huge moneymaking businesses. I mean, you can go online right now and buy a T-shirt, or a hat, or a stuffed animal with those dogs' pictures on them. I'm guessing that's how those dogs' owners make their living."

"Pepper and Jack aren't anywhere near that famous," I protested. "I think over a thousand likes is amazing, but don't these 'celebrity' pets get *millions* of likes? Besides, Relay's mostly just kids."

"I don't know that it takes millions of likes to start making money," Jai pointed out. "And I think you can do it on Relay. I knew a guy at my school back home who's a major sneaker head. He posts pics of his collection of kicks, and now he's got a sponsor. Last I heard he had like twenty-some thousand followers. He's making a lot of money—enough to buy more expensive sneakers."

"But she wouldn't be getting my log-in to take over the Relay account, even if she did get the dogs." My Frap seemed to churn in my stomach as I said those words out loud.

Nina leaned forward. "No, but she could use a super-similar handle, copy the hashtags from the most popular posts . . . I mean, this is the only thing that makes sense. Karen *must* be after the social media angle."

"If so, how can we prove it, though?" I asked.

Jai rubbed his temple. "The only thing I can think to do is for all of us to search Relay—use any kind of hashtags for West

Palm Beach and pugs. Or maybe she's tried to launch other dog or cat pages?"

"This is like looking for a needle in . . . a giant social media site," I said.

"That's a very weird metaphor, but yeah," Nina said.

"A weird *simile*," I corrected Nina, which I never got to do, but I couldn't even enjoy it thanks to the circumstances.

"In the meantime, I feel like I should have my dad call his friend—the lawyer?" Nina offered.

I nodded. "Maybe you should. I guess it can't hurt?"

I was tossing and turning in the trundle bed in Nina's room that night, still trying to fall asleep. Nina was fast asleep in her bed. I looked at my phone and my heart jumped when I saw a text from Jai.

I found a Relay account—I think it's her???

In the next text bubble there was a link, so I clicked it. It took me to an account for a Yorkshire terrier with the name @yolandayorkie. The account had over three thousand followers, but as I scrolled through the pictures they were all of a cute Yorkie posing—in a T-shirt, inside a giant teacup, on a beach. Why had Jai thought this was Karen's account, though?

And then I spotted it—Karen's face, cuddling with the Yorkie. I scrolled through the rest of the page. It was the only picture that included her face. How in the world had Jai even found this?

I texted back: **I see it!**

But what did Karen having this account even prove? Maybe she really was just an unpleasant person who was also a dog lover? I decided to go back to the start of her posts and look at the dates. She'd posted the first pic just last year. But the posts had stopped a few months ago.

I texted Jai again.

Thank you for finding this! How can we use to prove she's after the pugs to make $ though?

In her post on 5/17 last year she's trying to sell doggy T-shirts!! It says "link in profile" but she must have updated that because it's gone. But this at least proves she's into making $ thru posting.

I texted him back another thanks for finding the info and sat staring at Karen's page, hoping against hope that the info would be enough to convince my parents to continue fighting to keep Pepper and Jack.

I lay back down, unable to sleep, wishing I had Pepper and Jack there to snuggle beside me for comfort.

22

The End

When I got home the next morning, Mom was waiting with bad news. "Karen is coming back over this afternoon. With her mother."

I sank into a chair, my feet feeling too heavy to move.

The better news, Mom said, was that Aunt Maddie was driving back down to our house for the meeting. She really was the best. And when I called Nina to update her, she said her dad had spoken to his lawyer friend, and he would come over, too, which Mom and Dad said was fine. Nina and Jai also wanted to come, but Mom said no way. So they would both be on standby waiting to hear what happened.

I filled my parents in on the theory that the three of us had come up with, about Karen being out to find an established pet Relay account that she could potentially make money on. Mom and Dad seemed unsure, and made me promise to hear out Karen and her mother first.

The rest of the morning passed in a blur as Ollie and I tried to cram a lifetime's worth of doggy love into a couple of hours. We sat on the living room floor and played with Pepper and Jack as much as we could, but soon just started hugging and cuddling them. The poor pugs' fur got pretty wet, even though they kept trying to lick the tears from our faces. Aunt Maddie showed up, and then Mr. Evans, the lawyer, arrived.

Then there was a final knock on the door, and it was time.

Ollie, once again, took the dogs upstairs to his room. Maddie and I, Mr. Evans, and Dad gathered in the living room while Mom opened the door for Karen.

"This is my mom, Karla." Karen walked in and introduced a short woman wearing a denim skirt and a red T-shirt. She had shoulder-length brown hair, and didn't look much like Karen. But then again, I was looking for ways to prove she was a liar.

Karla was chewing gum so loudly you could hear the snap of her jaws. "Nice to meet cha," she said around the gum.

I was shifting from one foot to the other, unable to keep still.

"How nice, you must be home on leave," Dad told Karla. "Thank you for your service."

Karla nodded. "Sure thing." She sounded nervous. Right away I trusted her even less than Karen.

"What branch of the military do you serve in?" Dad asked.

Karla looked at Karen for a second, who ended up answering for her. "Marines. But let's get this done. I feel like this has all taken up too much of everyone's time."

"I think the Calloways were asking to hear the story of how the pugs were purchased by Karen's boyfriend, Ms. . . . what was your name again?" Mr. Evans, the lawyer, asked Karla.

"Johnson," Karen answered for Karla again.

"I'm sorry, I neglected to say, I'm Max Evans. I'm here on behalf of the Calloways."

"What, like their lawyer?" Karen's eyes grew round. She

looked from Dad to Mom. "I thought this was all going to be friendly."

"Not so far," Maddie, beside me, said under her breath. Mom, on her other side, nudged her younger sister.

Mom turned to Karla. "As we explained to your daughter the other day, we simply want to handle all this properly. You're a mother, so surely you understand that our children have grown very attached to these dogs over the past month. If they were to have to say goodbye . . ."

"It's not an *if* at this point," Karen broke in. "I've got the dogs' papers right here." She held out a manila folder, and after a few seconds, Mom took it from her.

Mom looked at them in silence for a few seconds. "I don't really know what I'm looking at here," Mom said, exasperation plain in her voice. "Will you take a look, Max?" she asked the lawyer.

"Although I'm not an expert on pedigree dogs, either, I did do some research into what AKC paperwork looks like, so I'll be happy to take a look," Max answered.

"In the meantime, Karla, perhaps you could tell us a little bit more about all the traveling that you and your daughter have been doing," Dad said.

Karla nodded, still cracking her gum periodically. "Sure. Well, like I'm sure she told you, those pups were a gift. From her boyfriend."

"That's not what we were asking," Dad interrupted.

Karla went on. "So anyway, we live over in the . . . north complex, and as you know, the buildings look identical. We think that's what happened."

A soft sigh escaped Dad's lips, then he tried again. "Okay, but the main issue here is the missing *time*. The part we can't wrap our heads around is what happened *after* the dogs were brought here by mistake. I mean, the dogs have been with us for more than a month at this point . . ."

Karla interrupted Dad. "So, see, that's my fault, is what it is. I got called away. Called overseas, really quick. No time to take care of any of my . . . affairs. I was supposed to tell her"—she jerked her head toward Karen—"about the dogs. But I didn't pass on the message."

"Melissa, Dan—could I have a word with you two for a

moment?" Mr. Evans cut in, nodding to Mom and Dad. "Excuse us," he said to Karen and Karla.

I turned to Maddie in panic, then tried to follow Mom, Dad, and Mr. Evans to the kitchen, but Mom shooed me away.

I couldn't hear what they were saying!

But, when they came back, I could tell from my parents' faces that it wasn't good news.

"Max says these papers seem to be in order," Dad said.

Mom gave me a helpless shrug.

Wait, what? Were we giving up so fast? What about the social media angle?

"No!" I cried.

"Honey, Max—Mr. Evans—says that since Karen has paperwork, and the dates seem to match the dogs' age, that at this point our only option would be to go to civil court," Mom said gently. "And without any paperwork on our end, he says our chances wouldn't be very good."

My heart was pounding so loud I felt like it was about to jump out of my chest. All of a sudden, the worst really was happening. How could this be it? How could I let Pepper and Jack go?

"Sweetie, it's probably best to get this over with quickly. Go on upstairs to say goodbye, and I'll get the dogs' things together." I knew Mom was serious, because tears were silently rolling down her cheeks when she said it.

I shook my head, rooted to the spot, unable to move. Dad came up and gently took my elbow. "Sam, sweetie, we've done all we could. But they have papers. And, I'm sorry, but we just can't afford to take this to court. I asked Max about the potential cost, and we just can't do it."

"But what about Relay . . . ?" I started.

Dad shook his head. "Max says that wouldn't hold up, not if they got the police involved, claiming we have her property." He gave me a little push toward the stairs, and I started walking, taking one step after the other. It was the longest walk of my life.

I reached Ollie's closed bedroom door, then took a deep breath before opening it. It felt like my lungs were full of tiny, sharp needles. I wasn't crying, not yet, but it was hard to breathe. Ollie took one look at my face and burst out crying. "No! I'm not giving up Pepper. I won't do it. She can come try to take her." He picked up Pepper so quickly she made a peeping sound in surprise, or protest. He held her tightly against him and went to the corner of the room, as though prepared to defend her when the strangers came upstairs.

I sat down on the floor and Jack ambled over to me. He looked up at me with those huge, black, trusting eyes. The image of him blurred in front of me as the tears started. I picked him up gently and held him close.

Why did they have to be such perfect little pugs anyway? If only they'd been mutts like Dipper . . . then there wouldn't be any pedigree papers.

"Wait a second," I said, putting Jack down and standing up. I looked at Ollie. "I'll be right back," I told him. "Maybe this isn't over."

I ran back down the stairs, this time taking them two or three at a time and almost falling on the landing.

Mom was packing up the dogs' bowls in a small shopping bag and Karen, Karla, Dad, and Mr. Evans were still gathered in the living room.

"I have something to say!" I announced. "I just realized—those papers she has *must* be fake, because these dogs aren't full-bred pugs, remember?" I asked Mom. "We found out at the vet. The vet tech, I think her name was Beth—yes, that's it! Beth, she's a pug breeder, and she said that Pepper and Jack were actually Frugs—part French bulldog!" I turned to Karen. "So, basically, I really don't see how you can have papers that say they're purebred pugs."

Karen's face and neck turned pink, then red. "They . . . we . . . I mean . . . Dave, my boyfriend, he must have been the victim of some kind of scam. He paid a lot of money for those puppies. He spent almost six grand . . ."

"I thought you said your boyfriend was Chris," I said.

"I'm going to stop you there," Maddie jumped in. "Pugs—even purebred—do not cost three grand a pop. Look it up. Besides, there's more here that stinks than just the papers and the money. Actually, it's kind of related to money, because the fact is that Karen here is looking to cash in on these pups being minor online celebrities. Their account has almost two thousand followers, and it's growing every day. That's just about the point where you can start to monetize."

Mr. Evans looked confused but interested. "You didn't mention the number of online followers when we spoke," he said to Dad. "And Maddie's right—I know from a recent case that people can make a lot of money from posting online—through sponsorships, and there are other revenue channels. But what I don't get is, how would Ms. Johnson here be able to take over an account that was started by your children?"

I raised my hand. "My friends and I thought about that. Someone could just change the username slightly, use all the same hashtags, follow the same people or accounts, and use pics of the same cute pups. It might take a little while, but definitely way less than starting from scratch." I turned to Karen once more. "And she needs a new way to promote her doggy T-shirts or whatever she sells, now that she's not posting as Yolanda the Yorkie anymore. What happened, did her real owners come back to claim her?"

Karen stood up. Her face was very red now. "She ran away!" she yelled at me. "Are you happy now? Is that what you want to hear?"

Maddie stood up. "What we want is to hear you admit that you've been lying, Karen. We want to hear you say you'll stop trying to take away these children's pets, that they've been caring for and loving for weeks and weeks. We also want to hear the sound of the door closing when you leave and never come back."

Karen opened her mouth as though to say something, but Maddie wasn't finished. "By the way, if that's *not* what we hear in the next two minutes—I hate to say it, but then *I'm* going to get involved. And I'm something way worse than a lawyer—I'm the aunt. I understand you're trying to launch some kind of online business, or maybe you just have a sponsorship deal you want to revive. Either way, you can kiss it all goodbye. I work in a very high-level position for a *very* large corporation. We have an extensive IT department, and one of my employees has already tracked your IP address through your previous account. He's poised and ready to use that information to track your activity going forward, even if you use a different computer. And what we'll do with that information is this: I run the social media for one branch of our company. I'm prepared to completely misuse my authority and use this account—at over three million followers, I've got a pretty big reach—to squash your little T-shirt business, to denounce you as a scam artist and a dog thief. So go ahead—take us to court. You'll find you can't use these dogs—or any other animal—to try to make a buck online. Ever again."

Wow. I stared at Maddie in awe. My aunt rocked!

Karen let out a huge sigh. "Fine. Whatever." She turned to Karla. "Come on, we're going."

"How could you go along with this? You should do a better job teaching your daughter responsibility," Mom told Karla in her best mom voice.

Karla snorted. "She's not my kid. She just paid me thirty bucks to come here."

I almost wanted to laugh, but then they were walking out the door, and I was just happy that they were leaving—*without* Pepper and Jack. I couldn't wait to hug those pups.

"Oh—Ollie!" I realized he was up in his room, probably still freaking out. I ran back up the stairs and yanked open his door. He was still in the corner holding both dogs. "It's okay! They're staying! I mean, the pugs—the people are gone—that Karen and her fake mother—they're gone!!! Pepper and Jack are stay-ing with us! It's over, Ollie!"

He seemed to melt in relief against the wall of his room, and I went over to him and gave him a hug that turned out to be pretty wet. My poor, sweet little brother who I'd once thought of as a slug. Now I could see how gentle his animal-loving heart really was.

I let him go after a few seconds, which he seemed pretty relieved about, and we sat down on the floor together and let the pugs run all over us. They seemed extra joyful now that we were so happy and relieved. I wondered if dogs could pick up on your emotions. It seemed pretty likely to me that they could. I looked up and saw Mom, Dad, Maddie, and Mr. Evans standing in the doorway, all smiling.

"Poor kids," Mom said. "You must still be so stressed after all this."

"Nah, Mom," I replied. "Actually, I read that having a dog makes you calmer; it even lowers your blood pressure."

"Oh, yeah? Where did you read that—no, wait, let me guess . . ."

"Online," Mom, Maddie, and I all said at the same time, and then we laughed.

"Maybe we need to rethink our household social media policy," Dad said.

"Well, for one thing, I'm definitely taking down the pugs' site. I'll keep my own—if I'm allowed," I added. "But no more celebrity pets around here. I just want pet-pets."

I held up Jack so that we were eye to eye. "You're staying with me, little guy—you and your sister!" He began to lick my entire face and I didn't mind the slobber one bit. The pugs were ours. Forever.

Except, said a little voice in my head, *since it wasn't Karen, who* did *leave the pugs on the porch? And will they ever come back?*

23

Aha!

Mom turned to Maddie. "So, was that really true, all that stuff you told Karen? About IT addresses and the IP guy and everything?"

Dad had walked Mr. Evans out, and Ollie was sitting on the floor playing with Pepper. I was holding Jack. I didn't want to let him go.

Maddie laughed. "It's an IT *guy* and IP *addresses*, but—no, that was pretty much all garbage. Your IP address even changes when you take your laptop to a coffee shop and log on. I was banking on her not understanding enough about computers to know that. Plus, I would never actually use my position that way. I just thought it sounded convincing."

"Impressive," Mom said. "What would I do without my little sister?" she added, side-hugging Maddie and laying her head on my aunt's shoulder.

"You'll never have to find out," Maddie told Mom, patting the top of her head. "But there's still one thing about all this that I don't get. Since Karen was lying, and those weren't really her pugs, and she basically admitted wanting to use their profile to make money, she must have found the pugs online. But how did she track them down to your *actual* address?" She glanced at me. "Like I said, you can't do that from an IP address."

Why hadn't I thought of that part before? I carefully put Jack on the floor and closed my eyes. My brain was chasing the tail of an idea that seemed just out of reach. I thought about how the *picture* of Karen had looked kind of familiar to me. When the real Karen had been at our house, threatening to take my dogs, I'd been too upset and wound up to notice, but . . .

"Aha! Kaitlyn!" I exclaimed. Maddie, Mom, and Ollie all turned to look at me. "That's got to be it—Kaitlyn Waters! She's a girl in my grade at school. She looks a *lot* like Karen, and I know Kaitlyn *does* have a sister who's in high school! Kaitlyn must have seen my pugs on Relay, and she probably told Karen that I had the pugs."

"Does this Kaitlyn girl know where you live?" Maddie asked me.

I nodded. "She came over for a slumber party with all the girls in my sixth-grade class."

"Kaitlyn Waters? But Karen said her last name was *Johnson*," Mom said.

"She *also* brought a random woman to your house and said she was her mother," Maddie pointed out.

"Good point," Mom said with a laugh. "Okay, now that that's over, I'm starving."

"For once, I don't feel like cooking," I said, stretching out beside Jack, who was, as usual, lying on his back waiting to have his belly scratched.

"We're not cooking," Mom declared. "We all deserve to just kick back and relax—and celebrate the pups staying with us. We're going out to dinner!"

"That sounds great, but I don't really feel like leaving them right now . . ." I kissed the soft, furry top of Jack's head. I really, truly got to keep him—and his sister—forever. It was definitely something to celebrate.

"Me neither," Ollie said, carrying Pepper and plopping her down beside her brother, then sitting down beside us.

"And I need to call Nina and Jai!" I burst out. In all of the excitement I'd forgotten my promise. "Can they come, too?"

"I have an idea," Maddie said. "Outdoor seating, puppy-friendly, and budget-friendly, too, since this dinner is the more the merrier!"

"Sounds good to me!" Dad said as he appeared in my doorway.

I called Nina and Jai to fill them in on everything. Then my parents, Maddie, Ollie, the pugs, and I hopped in the catering van. We picked up first Nina and then Jai, and then we drove to an inexpensive taco place in our neighborhood, with lots of picnic tables outside, and a great hot sauce bar that made both Jai and Nina very happy. They immediately started challenging each other to eat increasingly larger amounts of the different super-hot sauces.

"That one's not even hot," Jai said, after trying a sauce that came out of a pump decorated with a skeleton.

"I eat stuff this hot for breakfast," Nina countered. "Let's try the next one. You in, Sam?"

I snuck Pepper a bite of chicken under the table. "No way. I'm not endangering my taste buds with a megadose of capsaicin."

"What even is that?" Jai asked, lowering the tortilla chip he'd been about to crunch.

"It's the hot stuff in peppers," Nina said. "Sam just likes to show off her big, fancy cooking words."

"Okay, good to know," Jai said with a grin, then ate the chip loaded with capsaicin. I cringed, thinking about the burn.

"Nobody let the dogs lick anything with hot sauce!" I said. "They'll get sick."

"I won't," Ollie said solemnly. "Promise."

Jack lapped from the water bowl we'd put by the table, and I yawned. "I'm tired," I said, shaking my head. "I haven't been sleeping much."

"Aww, I'm sorry this has been so hard on you, Sam," Mom said to me. "I wish now we'd just sent that girl away from the start. But at first it seemed at least possible she was telling the truth."

"I know it did—that's what kept costing me sleep. It's not your fault. If it's anybody's, it's mine. I shouldn't have turned the pugs into minor online celebrities."

Maddie was about to take a sip of her iced tea, but set the cup down and gave me a serious look. "Sam, you didn't do anything wrong. You were posting cute pictures of your dogs. You didn't share your address, or do anything at all that was out of line. Just because someone else tried to take advantage of you, that doesn't mean you were in the wrong. It's also not your fault one of your classmates has a horrible big sister."

"I'm not the world's biggest fan of Kaitlyn, either," I grumbled, biting down on a chip.

"Your aunt's right, Sam," Dad agreed. "You have to be as responsible as you can, but you also can't let the fact that there are scammers and liars out there make you afraid."

I nodded. "Thanks, Dad. I mean it." I turned to look at them all. "Mom, Dad, and Aunt Maddie—you all really clinched it in the end. I'm so grateful you even let me keep the pups in the first place. And I'm really lucky to have parents—and an aunt—who'll fight for me, for us, to keep them."

"You're welcome, sweetie," Mom said, and then the serious moment was over because Nina must have finally reached her hot sauce tolerance level. Jai jumped over Jack as he ran to get her some ice.

"Do you want my ice?" Maddie asked her as she fanned her hands in front of her mouth.

"No!" Nina squawked out.

"He should get her some kind of milk," I said. "Ice won't help a capsaicin burn." I got up and followed Jai to the counter. The restaurant didn't have milk, but they did give us a big bowl of sour cream.

Nina ate a few globs. "Better, but my throat still hurts. Maybe you were right about the sauce," Nina finally croaked out.

"I am a food genius," I told her.

"And very modest," Jai added.

"Well, that's the best part about me," I said. "I'm more than just one thing." Even though I was basically kidding, I also knew there was some truth to that. The improv retreat had gone well—and if Nina did start a forensics club, maybe I'd sign up for that, too. After all, I'd shown some pretty good detective skills today in figuring out the Frug clue!

"Hey, so now that everything's settled with the pugs, I kind of have some news," Jai told me.

"Please tell me it's good news?" I asked, crossing my fingers.

"I think so. There are two things, actually. First, my uncle's driving me to Silver Spring tomorrow. I'm going to get Dipper so he can stay with me this year."

I grinned. "That's amazing news! I can't wait to meet him— and for him to be best friends with Pepper and Jack!"

Jai laughed. "Me neither."

"So what's the second thing?" Nina asked.

"My dad took me to enroll in my new school today. And, well, it's *your* school!"

My heart jumped. "That's even more amazing!" I exclaimed, and hugged him before remembering that my parents, Nina, and Maddie were all staring at me (the pugs were too distracted by taco crumbs to care).

I pulled away, face pink, but still grinning.

24

The Pug Twins

This time it was Pepper who noticed the feet first.

There were two sets, both in sneakers. Ollie and I were home with the pugs while our parents were out running errands. I was making Ollie watch *Whose Line Is It Anyway?* with me as improv comedy training, and threatening to make him join the In-Betweeners when he got up to middle school.

Pepper barked, and Jack joined in, so my brother and I went out on to the porch to investigate. But the sneakers we'd spotted were gone. "Hello?" I called, looking around. And then two little kids—a boy and a girl, both red-haired with freckles—came running around from the other side of the building.

"Hi," the boy said breathlessly.

"Do we know you?" I asked.

"Caden, right?" Ollie asked. The boy nodded.

"We used to ride our bikes around together some," Ollie told me. "Didn't you move away, though?" he asked Caden.

Caden nodded. "Yep. In May. Our mom came back today to get some stuff she left."

"Is this your sister?" I asked him.

He nodded. "This is Chloe."

The girl, I noticed, was looking down at her feet. Her face was pink.

"Are you guys twins?" I asked.

Caden nodded. Neither of them was looking up at us now. They both kept staring at their sneakers.

A pair of twins who couldn't quite meet our eyes. Back in the house, I heard Pepper and Jack barking. Hmm. I had a thought.

"Wait a second—you moved in May?" I asked, remembering

the day I'd found the pugs in their blanket. "Did you—did you leave a pair of pugs on our porch?"

Chloe nodded. "Uh-huh."

"What?" Ollie cried.

"We had to leave really fast," Caden explained. "We . . . our mom left our stepdad, and she said we couldn't bring them. The dogs."

"We were going to stay with our mom's friend, and she's allergic." Chloe met my eyes for the first time. "Caden said he knew your family was nice, and that Ollie loved dogs."

"Our mom was going to take them to a shelter," Caden put in. "We didn't want that. We just wanted them to have a good home."

I thought back to everything I'd done to try to keep the same thing from happening to the pugs, and I couldn't be mad at these twins, not even a little bit. Besides, they were even younger than Ollie. And it sounded like they were having a really rough summer. My heart broke for them, thinking about how they had had to do what I was so afraid to—give up the pugs.

"We can't take them back," Chloe said. Her voice sounded sad. "We just wanted to see them, for a minute, maybe. Just say hi and see that they're okay."

"We are taking really good care of them," I told her. "I'm glad you left them with us. And of course you can say hi."

Ollie and I went inside and brought the dogs out on the porch. The pugs wagged their tails at the sight of their previous owners. Chloe and Caden gave each dog a hug and patted their ears.

"We missed you, Mickey," Chloe told Jack.

"And you, Minnie," Caden whispered to Pepper.

"Wait a second, did you name them Minnie and Mickey?" I asked the twins.

Chloe nodded. "We used to live in Orlando, and we love Disney."

"We do, too," Ollie said.

"Mickey and Minnie are great names, but we didn't know, so we named them Pepper and Jack," I explained.

"That's cute, too," Chloe said.

"Caden! Chloe!" a woman's voice called out across the parking lot.

"We have to go," Chloe said sadly, passing Jack, aka Mickey, back to me. Reluctantly, Caden handed Pepper to Ollie.

"Thanks for . . . I'm glad you guys are taking care of them." Caden swiped at his eyes with the back of his hand.

He and Chloe waved to the dogs and to us, and then they were racing toward their mom, across the parking lot.

"We just met the real pug twins," I told Ollie. "I guess that's the last mystery solved."

"I feel sad for them," Ollie told me.

"Me too," I said. "We have to make these little guys super happy. Since Caden and Chloe trusted us to."

"We were going to do that anyway," Ollie pointed out.

I put my arm around my little brother, who, surprisingly, didn't pull away. "I know we were. But we'll think about the twins now, too, when we do."

Two Months Later

25

The First Rule

"Are you ready?" Nina asked me as we stood backstage, hand in hand, seconds away from my very first improv comedy show. We'd been rehearsing for a month, but now that the moment was finally here, my palms felt sweaty, and I wondered if I had the guts to actually go out there and do it. But then I remembered my first day at the comedy retreat, when I'd learned that the first rule of improvisational comedy is that the answer is always yes. Whatever suggestion the audience throws out, whatever happens onstage—you have to make the best of it, find a way to find the funny. Just say yes. So how could I say anything else at this moment?

"Yes," I told Nina, and she squeezed my hand.

"You're going to slay," she promised. I heard our advisor, Ms. Miller, introducing us all by name, and I had to let go of Nina's hand and step forward first; we were going alphabetically.

I walked onstage, feeling the bright lights hot on my face, and took my place in line with the rest of my team. Nina came out a few moments later, but she stood in the front to introduce the first sketch and interact with the audience, since she was our team captain.

"So for this first game, we need your help," she told the audience. I tried not to think about the fact that everyone who was important to me who wasn't already on this stage was out there: my parents, my little brother, my aunt Maddie . . . and Jai.

"First, we need a suggestion of a country," Nina announced.

Lots of people called out names of countries, but some of the loudest I heard were "Canada!" "Mexico!" and "India!" I wondered if Jai had been the one to yell India. He was still saving for his trip there, and we talked about it all the time. And he'd promised to be a loud participant from the audience tonight.

Nina picked Canada, then asked for suggestions of jobs. I heard a bunch of normal ones: nurse, lawyer, teacher—and a few weird ones like shepherd, underwater hotel manager, and professional sleeper. Nina went with the last one—if it were me, I might have picked underwater hotel manager.

When the skit started, it was slow going at first, probably because we all kept having to take turns being professional sleepers and trying out new spots on the stage. Then Ms. Miller called a freeze, and yelled out "Western!" That meant we were all supposed to continue the scene but have it be part of an old Western movie.

I felt like I could do this since my dad is obsessed with those old movies. "Where in the Sam Hill is my horse?" I called in my best cowboy accent. "What in tarnation is going on here? I paid these people good money to watch my horse while I went to sleep."

I heard a laugh from the audience, which made me smile.

Then Mark Wilson pretended to wake up. "We're professional sleepers! We thought you said you were paying *us* to sleep while *you* watched your horse!" That also got a laugh from the audience, and then we were rolling again. We changed to teen vampire drama, and then Shakespeare, before resetting for our second game.

Before I knew it, the show was over, and the audience was standing up and clapping. I felt like I couldn't stop grinning. Being a part of the improv comedy team was exhilarating. I didn't love it as much as cooking—and I was pretty sure I wasn't quite as good at it, either—but it felt great to try something that I used to be so scared of.

Then the stage lights dimmed and we all started walking out to join our families. Mom and Dad and Maddie gave me hugs, and Ollie even said, "That was cool," which was high praise, coming from my brother.

Then Jai was walking toward me, carrying a bundle of brightly colored flowers. He picked me up and twirled me around and I laughed in surprise—but also at that moment I felt wonderfully, perfectly happy. "You were great up there!" he said, putting me down and handing me the flowers. "But then, I knew you would be."

"That makes one of us," I said with a small laugh.

Standing there, so close to Jai, with him wearing one of the suits he usually wore to perform and me holding the flowers he'd just given me—suddenly I felt nervous around him. There was a fluttering in my stomach, and my palms as I held the bouquet felt sweaty.

"I have something to ask you," Jai said, looking down at me. He really was very tall. And very cute. I looked up into his warm brown eyes and nodded.

He took a step closer to me. "Sam, I really like you. A lot. I want to make it—make *us*—official. What I'm asking is, Sam . . . will you be my girlfriend?"

My face broke out into another grin. For the second time in the night, I stuck to the first and most important rule of improv: always say yes.

* * *

For our first official date, I asked Jai's dad to help me track down the perfect recipe. I'd assembled all the ingredients, but the plan was for Jai and me to cook the dish together.

My mom dropped the pugs and me off at Dr. Jams's house. "His father will be there?" Mom asked again.

"Yes," I said. "He's going to be right downstairs in the media room, but he's letting us cook—and eat, if it turns out okay, before coming back up."

"What do you mean, 'if it turns out'? Everything you make is delicious."

"Aw, thanks, Mom. Right back at you. But this dish is definitely outside my area of expertise."

"You'll have to learn to make every kind of cuisine in cooking school, so why not start now?" Mom pulled into a parking space. I picked up the pups' travel crate with one hand and the bag of ingredients with the other.

"Are you sure you want to bring them?" Mom asked. "I can take them back with me."

"No way. Besides, Jai's dog is there now, too. It's a puppy party!"

"Okay, text your dad when you're ready to be picked up. Before ten," she added with an arched eyebrow.

"Of course. Thanks, Mom." I stepped out of the car and pointed to the pugs in the crate. "Thank you for—everything this summer."

"You're welcome, kid," Mom said. "Good luck with the vindaloo."

Jai met me at the elevator and took the dogs' crate from me. "Hey, Sam!"

"Hey!"

"So what's this surprise dish?" he asked as I followed him inside the condo.

"Hey, Dipper!" I sat down on the kitchen floor to give Jai's dog a proper greeting. Then I opened the pugs' crate and was absolutely covered in excited dog.

I giggled as Jack and Pepper barked at Dipper and the three of them played together like old friends. I sat in the middle of them, enjoying the furry fun.

"I guess I'll just wait," Jai said with a mock sigh as he leaned against the kitchen counter.

"Sorry." I stood up. "I'm actually pretty excited to tell you about it. Can you hand me the bag I brought?"

He did, and I rooted around until I found what I was looking for. Jai's dad had translated the recipe for me, but I'd saved the one Jai's grandmother had sent from Mumbai. "Here's what we're making. You said you wanted to learn."

Jai held the recipe in his hands for a few moments, then looked up at me. His eyes looked suspiciously bright. "From my grandmother? You arranged this?"

I nodded. "I've been doing some research, and even though it's a little complicated, I bet we can figure it out. I found all the ingredients, I think. Do you want to get started?"

Jai smiled. "I do. Thank you, Sam—this is so cool."

I started unpacking the ingredients. "I thought it would be good if you got in some practice now, and then you can cook with your grandmother when you get to visit."

"You're the best," Jai said, giving me a huge hug. I laughed, and Jack decided that this was a game he should be involved in and started circling around us, and then Dipper and Pepper followed him.

Jai and I both laughed, but before letting go, Jai leaned in and kissed me. All three dogs were pressed against our legs, but I didn't mind.

"Thanks for doing this. I can't wait to cook with you."

"Me neither," I told him. "No matter how the dish turns out, we've already hit my triple threat."

"Oh yeah?" Jai said with a grin.

I nodded. "I have all three of my favorites: cooking, dogs . . . and you. It's the perfect day."

Jai leaned in and gave me another kiss. Then I handed him a clove of garlic. "Peel this."

"Yes, Chef," Jai said with a wink.

"I like the sound of that," I told him. Jack gave a short bark, as though he was agreeing. Jack really gets me.

I leaned down and whispered in his ear. "I love you. Don't forget, okay?"

Then I could have sworn Jack gave me a wink, too.

Acknowledgments

Just like a chef can't bring the diner a delicious dish without the help of everyone from the grocer to her sous chef, a writer doesn't cook up a book all alone. As always, a huge thank you to Suzie, Cassandra, Devin, and all the folks at New Leaf.

Aimee Friedman and Olivia Valcarce, it has been great revisiting the world of Wish Pugs with you guys!

My friends Nikki and Gabriella—thank you once again for being my sounding boards, readers, and cheerleaders.

Speaking of cheer, thanks to my family of friends for always being there for me, and especially to my mom for always being there to hear about my day.

A big bulldog shout-out to my work family at PBDA. Thanks again, Sarah, for bringing me on board.

And finally, once again, thanks to my students for being my

inspiration—*and* helping me name the pugs . . . especially Colin M. this time, who came up with Pepper and Jack!

Most of all, this book is for Nina. Everyone should have a best friend—or a student—like you. We miss you but your light still shines.

Can't get enough of puppy love?

Be sure to read:

Find more reads you will love . . .

Bria Muller isn't happy about being stuck on her aunt and uncle's dairy farm for the summer. There is one thing she's good at: crafting towering, over-the-top milkshakes like the ones she loved back home. But everyone seems to think Bria is just a snobby city girl, including her cousins' cute friend, Gabe. With the family business in danger of being sold, can Bria's shakes make a difference . . . and will she ever fit into country life?

Have you read all the (Wish) books?

☐ *Clementine for Christmas* by Daphne Benedis-Grab

☐ *Carols and Crushes* by Natalie Blitt

☐ *Allie, First at Last* by Angela Cervantes

☐ *Gaby, Lost and Found* by Angela Cervantes

☐ *Sit, Stay, Love* by J. J. Howard

☐ *Pugs and Kisses* by J. J. Howard

☐ *Pugs in a Blanket* by J. J. Howard

☐ *The Boy Project* by Kami Kinard

☐ *Best Friend Next Door* by Carolyn Mackler

☐ *11 Birthdays* by Wendy Mass

☐ *Finally* by Wendy Mass

☐ *13 Gifts* by Wendy Mass

☐ *The Last Present* by Wendy Mass

☐ *Graceful* by Wendy Mass

☐ *Twice Upon a Time: Beauty and the Beast, the Only One Who Didn't Run Away* by Wendy Mass

☐ *Twice Upon a Time: Rapunzel, the One with All the Hair* by Wendy Mass

☐ *Twice Upon a Time: Sleeping Beauty, the One Who Took a Really Long Nap* by Wendy Mass

☐ *Blizzard Besties* by Yamile Saied Méndez

☐ *Playing Cupid* by Jenny Meyerhoff

☐ *Cake Pop Crush* by Suzanne Nelson

☐ *Macarons at Midnight* by Suzanne Nelson

☐ *Hot Cocoa Hearts* by Suzanne Nelson

☐ *You're Bacon Me Crazy* by Suzanne Nelson

☐ *Donut Go Breaking My Heart* by Suzanne Nelson

☐ *Sundae My Prince Will Come* by Suzanne Nelson

☐ *I Only Have Pies for You* by Suzanne Nelson

☐ *Shake It Off* by Suzanne Nelson

☐ *Confectionately Yours: Save the Cupcake!* by Lisa Papademetriou

☐ *My Secret Guide to Paris* by Lisa Schroeder

☐ *Sealed with a Secret* by Lisa Schroeder

☐ *Switched at Birthday* by Natalie Standiford

☐ *The Only Girl in School* by Natalie Standiford

☐ *Once Upon a Cruise* by Anna Staniszewski

☐ *Deep Down Popular* by Phoebe Stone

☐ *Revenge of the Flower Girls* by Jennifer Ziegler

☐ *Revenge of the Angels* by Jennifer Ziegler